What Goes Around

By Katrina Avant

This book is a work of fiction and does not depict any person living or dead. The characters were created from the imagination of the author.

What Goes Around...

Katrina Avant

Chapter 1

Dain stood across the ballroom, watching Jayden bully men away from his sister. He was attending Anderson and Paige's wedding reception.

"I believe that's my cue." Dain grinned at the men scattering to the four corners of the room. He silently thanked Jayden for clearing the path so he could introduce himself to the lovely Mia formally.

Taking the last swallow from his drink, and placing the empty glass on a nearby table, Dain was just about to cross the room, when his sister stepped into his path.

"Where do you think you're going, little brother?" Dani asked her twin. At six feet five, two hundred thirty well-toned pounds, he was by no means "little". She was only a few minutes older than Dain, but she always pulled rank when she knew he was about to do something stupid. And Dain's desire to approach Mai was at the top of that list.

Dain sighed his frustration. "Dani, what do you want?" He was more than annoyed with his over-protective sister. He was on a mission and wasn't going to let her or anyone else discourage him in his pursuit of Mia Stone.

"I know what you're thinking, and that is NOT a good idea. Mia is off-limits Dain, you know this. Jayden will have your head if you even think about approaching his sister," she reminded him.

"I am just going over there to introduce myself that's all and—" Dain started.

"That is never all with you," she quipped, cutting him off with a sneer.

Dani knew her brother as well as she knew herself. Although they were fraternal twins, she could still read his thoughts, and at the moment, those thoughts were somewhere in the vicinity of him bedding Mia. She loved her brother, but he was a notorious womanizer who had a tendency to get himself into a world of trouble when it came to women.

Dain loved his sister, but sometimes she could be a bit intrusive in his opinion. Sure, he loved women and sometimes his love for them got him into trouble, but he could handle himself. He was always able to soothe hurt feelings when his interest in the woman of the month came to an end, and as far as he was concerned, Mia Stone would be no different.

Dain Sinclair was a pilot for a major airline and met many women on his trips around the globe. He believed in wining and dining as many women as he possibly could, and if all involved enjoyed themselves, what could be the harm? Besides, he made sure that each of the women he dated understood his number one rule upfront—no commitments. Yes, there were those who were determined to change his mind, hence the trouble.

"I'm only going to say this once more, Mia is off limits. She is not your usual type. You know the ones, skanky and desperate. STAY AWAY FROM HER!" Dani made her point by punctuating each of her words with a poke of her finger to his chest. Hoping she made her point, she gave her brother the evil eye before joining her date, multimillionaire Devin Powers.

Rolling his eyes at his sister's antics, Dain turned his attention back to where he last spotted Mia, only to discover that she wasn't there. Scanning the room in hopes of finding her, he was disappointed that she was nowhere to be found. Disappointed, he retrieved a glass of champagne from the tray of a passing server. He couldn't believe he missed his opportunity all because of his sister.

Accepting his misfortune, Dain left the ballroom to call one of the many women who were always on standby for moments like this. He did not intend to spend the rest of the evening alone in a hotel room.

#

After making sure that Mia was out of harm's way, Jayden continued to scan the room for more wolves who might have plans for his sister. He spotted Dani Sinclair having what appeared to be a heated conversation with her brother Dain. From the expression on Dain's face, he would hate to be the one on the receiving end of that tongue-lashing.

"I wonder what did he do...jeez," Jayden commented, before turning away from them, in search of his date.

"Hey baby, I see you have thoroughly cleared the room tonight," Andee noted with a chuckle when he joined her.

"Yeah, and if they know what's good for them, they will stay clear. Every one of those guys was up to no good," he added with a frown. Jayden was determined to protect his sister from any man who would use her.

"Jayden, Mia is a grown woman who's capable of handling herself. She has done quite well so far without you." Andee pointed out.

"Well, I'll be there to give her some extra backup. Now that she has her brothers, there is no reason for her to have to deal with these thirsty assholes alone anymore," Jayden replied, still eyeing the room for predators.

Andee rolled her eyes. Jayden and his brother Anderson had only recently discovered they had a sister, fathered by their absentee father Rendell Stone.

"Okay, but you're relieved from guard duty because Mia left. So can I please have some time with my man?" Andee liked Mia, but she was glad she left. She wanted them to enjoy themselves.

Jayden gave the ballroom a final sweep. Satisfied Mia had left for the evening Jayden led Andee to the dance floor. Now he could really have a good time.

In the lobby, Dain was scrolling through the names on his phone, when one of the wedding guests sashayed passed him. He spotted her well-endowed behind before he noticed the rest of her. He had glimpsed the woman briefly at the ceremony, before locking onto Mia Stone. Dain had completely forgotten about her, but now here was that beautiful bottom again.

"Ah, excuse me, Miss," Dain called out, drawing the woman's attention, "weren't you at the wedding?" He continued.

Taylor Patterson, the groom's cousin, turned towards the man who had gotten her attention. "Yes I was at the wedding," she replied hesitantly, eyeing Dain suspiciously. Taylor had seen his type in action before and had no intentions of being one of the many toys in this man's collection.

Grinning widely, Dain placed his phone back into his jacket pocket, confident that he would not be needing it tonight. Sizing the woman up, he let his eyes caress her from head to toe. She was gorgeous. Her sun-kissed skin glowed with health. Her thick, layered hair brushed the tops of her bare shoulders along with a pair of exquisitely designed earrings that perfectly complimented her figure-hugging gown. Her hazel eyes were slightly overshadowed by her high cheekbones and small pouty mouth. Having touched every other portion of her body with his eyes, Dain's gaze skidded to a stop at her C-cupped breasts. Mentally he licked his lips.

After watching this man shamelessly use his eyes to roam her body, Taylor cleared her throat to get his attention. "Is there something that you want to say to me, or did you forget while staring at my boobs?" She asked, folding her arms with a deepening frown.

Having been sidetracked as to why he stopped the woman, Dain pulled his attention back to the mission at hand—getting her into his bed. "Um, I'm sorry…how rude of me."

"Yes, it was rude," Taylor agreed, still frowning.

Catching the disdain in the woman's voice, Dain finally comprehended that she was not flattered by his attention. In fact, upon closer inspection, he realized that she was angry. His brows rose in surprise. He was not used to women rebuffing his interests. Whenever he turned his attention to any woman, she usually fell all over herself making sure that she kept that attention. However, this woman was upset. This was a new experience for Dain.

"I was wondering if you would like to come up to my room for a drink and some conversation." Dain plowed forward, despite his growing unease. He did not know how to handle this situation; a situation he was unfamiliar with and he didn't like it.

"Let me see," Taylor pretended to ponder. "Let's forget that I don't know you or that you didn't even bother to ask my name…and oh, that you just practically molested me visually," she recounted full of sarcastic indignation.

"Mister, there is no way in hell that I would have a drink or anything else with you. So piss off!" Taylor, having had her fill of Dain, turned on her heels and walked away, berating him with each angry step.

Stunned, Dain could only watch the irate woman's retreating figure as she stomped away from him. He didn't know what to make of it. What had he done wrong? He stood there for a full two minutes just staring at the space the gorgeous woman had vacated. Finally snapping out of it, he decided he needed another drink and headed for the bar.

#

Mia, having witnessed the scene between Dain and Taylor, chuckled softly from her vantage point across the lobby. She was about to leave when she spotted Dain scrolling through his phone. She first noticed him during the wedding and then at the reception. She also noticed he found interest in her. This made her smile. Mia had an appetite for handsome men and planned to make a meal of the delightfully handsome Dain. While Jayden was busy scaring away the other men, she watched his attempt to cross the room in her direction. Unfortunately, his sister got to him first.

Chuckling, Mia watched a frustrated Dain head to the bar. Because of her plans for the night, she decided against following him. Unfortunately, she had already snagged her entertainment for the evening and did not want to keep him waiting. But next time she would clear her calendar to treat herself to Dain Sinclair's fabled goodies.

Chapter 2

After being shot down by the woman in the lobby, Dain had a couple of drinks in the bar and then headed up to his room. Certain, that he would be spending the evening with a lucky wedding attendee, he had optimistically booked a suite for the evening. He lived in the city but never entertained women there. This was a deliberate plan of self-preservation. If things went badly with any of the women he bedded, he did not want them to show up to his home to extract any form of retaliation.

Letting himself into his suite, Dain, frustrated loosened his tie and placed the do not disturb placard on the outer door handle. After Taylor's snub, he wasn't in the mood for company of any kind. Still puzzled by her rejection, he immediately consulted the nearest mirror to peer at his reflection. Yes, he was still handsome. He gazed into clear brown eyes, moving from there to his smooth dark skin.

Next, his eyes turned to his close-cropped hair, which was groomed to perfection. Unbuttoning his crisp white dress shirt, he lifted the equally white undershirt to reveal the results of hours spent in his home gym. His upper body was ripped to flawlessness. Satisfied that his body displayed the evidence of the care he provided it, Dain lowered the undershirt. He could not understand why Taylor rejected him. Shrugging out of the dress shirt, he moved to the bar making himself another drink to ponder the answer.

#

Returning to the ballroom to say her goodbyes to some of the guests, Taylor was still fuming over the obnoxiously arrogant man she encountered in the lobby. She could not believe the audacity of the man. Did he expect her to fall at his feet or something? What an idiot, she thought.

"Hey Taylor, what's the matter?" Jayden asked his cousin. "You look mad enough to fight."

"Some idiot practically molested me in the lobby, is all," Taylor answered with angry exaggeration. Even though Dain never laid a hand on her, she felt violated just the same.

"What? Where is he? I'll take care of him!" Equally angry, Jayden tried to maneuver around Taylor, heading to the lobby to beat some sense into the fool.

Grabbing his arm, Taylor stopped him. "It's ok Jayden, I put a stop to his nonsense. He didn't touch me, he just made me feel as if he had. Besides, you need to tone it down some. I saw how you handled that crew of misfits that swarmed Mia," she added with a chuckle.

"Yeah, well, obviously I didn't get my point across clearly enough, because I'm sure the guy harassing you was one of the clowns I scared away earlier," he told Taylor while still surveying the room.

"Anyway, I just came back to let you know that I'm heading home," Taylor informed him.

"Come on; let me walk you to your car, just in case that guy decides to give you a repeat performance. This time he *will* get the message." Jayden placed his hand on her back, guiding her from the ballroom.

****

Mia rose from the bed fully sated. The romp with her latest plaything had been a real treat. Satisfied for the moment, she would have liked to have rolled around with Dain Sinclair instead. Now that would have been the icing on the evening, she thought. Smiling, she reached for her dress that had been tossed on a nearby chair.

"Hey, where are you going?" Her bed partner asked her. "I thought we would make a night of it. I was hoping I could get to know you," he added reaching for her.

"Not tonight love, maybe another time," she stated, pulling on her shoes.

Mia hated when they became clingy. And considering she just met the man at her brother's wedding, he had no right to be whining about her leaving. Blowing him a kiss before leaving his bedroom, Mia made her way to the front door; letting herself out to head home.

Reaching her car, she hit the door locks and got behind the wheel. Before securing her seatbelt, Mia reached into her purse for her phone. As she suspected, Jayden had called several times.

Mia sighed. "I better let him know I'm alright before he comes looking for me." She appreciated her brother's newfound concern for her well-being, but she was a big girl who could take care of herself. With Jayden's strong-arming, she was just grateful he hadn't had the opportunity to scare away her latest conquest.

After reassuring her brother that he didn't have to come to her rescue, Mia started her car and headed home.

Thinking back on Dain, she knew he wanted her, she could see it in his eyes. She knew that look, a look that she encountered often. She smiled when she thought about how he just switched gears when she became unavailable. He just moved on to the next attractive body, something she often did when her target became unobtainable.

Yes, 'what's his name' filled in quite nicely. Her body still tingled from the encounter. Oh well, with her true conquest delayed, she was certain she would have her chance with Dain at another time. She would make sure of it.

Chapter 3

Rendell Stone finally returned to his suite, after skulking around his son's wedding and reception unobserved. He wished he had been a part of his family's joyous occasion. They all seemed so happy, so pleased. They went on about their lives as if he didn't exist, as if he never existed. He thought he should have been sitting right next to Adaisha, sharing in the joyous occasion. They should have been experiencing the event together as a family. However, he was forced to hide in the shadows while his son and new bride took their vows on that beautiful sunny afternoon.

Despite being an outcast at his oldest son's wedding, in his son's life, Rendell still felt joy and a little pride at Anderson's choice of a bride. He had done some research on Miss Paige Bennett and found she was everything that she appeared to be. He knew that he had no right, but he had to make sure that his son had made a wise choice. He cringed at the thought of Anderson making the wrong decision as he had with Mia's mother, Miranda.

During the ceremony, Rendell noticed he wasn't the only one who was forced to be on the outside looking in.

He observed an expensively dressed young woman, who also appeared to be there to witness the happy couple's union. He didn't know who she was, but she seemed relieved once the officiant pronounced the couple's union as man and wife. Although curious, he could not chance being discovered, so he did not approach her to inquire as to why she was there.

Sighing, Rendell dropped into one of the room's armchairs, weary from the day's festivities. Tired as he was, he tried formulating a plan to win his family back. He knew he had to overcome hurt feelings and years of resentment, but there had to be a way to make that happen. After being rebuffed by his eldest son and his ex-wife, he felt his best option would be to approach his youngest son. Jayden was his last hope. If he wouldn't accept him, Rendell knew he would lose his family forever.

Rendell wanted his entire family back, not just his sons but his wife too. He noticed during the ceremony, that Adaisha was unescorted at the wedding, which meant in his mind that she was unattached. He felt her being single would make it easier for him to win her back. With a strategy forming, he rose to prepare for bed. He had to get some rest before he executed his plan.

#

Anastasia Stanton-Graham stared out the window of her limo on the ride back to the airport. It was finally over. Now maybe she and Justin could have a real marriage. Her father had begged her to divorce him after that fiasco in Aruba, but she couldn't. Justin was who she wanted, for better or worse. Besides, she had invested too much time and money in him to give up now, not to mention they had a child together.

Anastasia thought back to that awful morning when she got the phone call from her father, informing her that her beloved husband and been arrested in Aruba. She hadn't known he had left Metro City let alone the country. After she was informed of Justin's arrest, she took one of her family's private jets and flew down to the island to bail her husband out of jail. Accompanied by her attorney, she had marched right into the police station, demanding his release.

Her father hadn't known exactly why Justin had been arrested; at least that was what he had told her. Anastasia was taken aback when the officer in charge informed her that Justin had been arrested for breaking into

Paige Bennett's suite and assaulting the woman's fiancé.
Paige was Justin's former girlfriend.

Anastasia was devastated. She knew her husband
still had feelings for Paige, but she had no idea that he
would go this far with his obsession with her. The evening
after their wedding, Anastasia had made it clear to Justin
that part of his life with Paige was over and she was his
wife now. She thought he had understood the ground rules
and gotten over his little crush, but apparently not.

After Justin's release, her attorney had smoothed
things over with the local authorities and they had flown
home. During the flight, Anastasia laid down the law
concerning their marriage and the cold hard facts of the
consequences if he did not comply. She firmly stipulated
that Paige Bennett was off limits or she would ruin him to
the point that he would be blacklisted the world over.
Anastasia believed that she had finally gotten her point
across. However, she needed reassurance that Paige was no
longer a threat to her marriage, so she secretly attended the
wedding.

The ceremony was underway by the time she
arrived. She had witnessed the happy occasion discretely
hidden behind one of the columns in the sanctuary. Paige

Bennett was now Paige Stone, happily married to the love of her life.

Anastasia had breathed a deep sigh of relief. No matter what happened now, she knew Anderson Stone would make sure Paige was safe and secure from Justin Graham.

With her reassurance of Paige's status, she had turned to leave when she noticed an elderly man also observing the happy couple's day. She assumed he was an uninvited guest as well. Not caring who he was and needing to leave before being discovered, Anastasia left the church, heading home to her new life with her properly submissive husband.

****

Adaisha stood in the shower, letting the warm water flow over her body. She happily smiled at the thought of Anderson and Paige's wedding. It was beautiful and she was glad at least one of her sons had found bliss. Although she knew Jayden was taken with Andee, she just didn't see the same light in his eyes that she saw in Anderson's when it came to Paige. She wanted both her sons to be as happy as she was.

"There you are. I am so sorry I was unable to make Anderson's wedding."

Adaisha smiled at her new husband joining her in the shower. Matthew took the soap from her and proceeded to lather her body with it. She and Matthew had been an item for over three years. A match both of her sons approved of. However, Jayden and Anderson were unaware that the two had been married for two weeks. She was now Mrs. Adaisha Cabot. Not wanting to take away from Anderson and Paige's day by announcing their nuptials, she and Matthew had agreed to announce their happy news when the honeymooning couple returned home.

"Not a problem baby, I knew your absence could not be helped. Both the boys asked about you. They love you too you know," Adaisha smiled up at her new husband.

"And I love them as if they were my sons," Matthew replied, kissing his wife.

In an attempt to change the subject, Matthew gripped Adaisha tighter, molding her into his body. "I've missed you," he whispered to an aroused Adaisha.

Moaning, Adaisha kissed him as he showed her how much.

Chapter 4

"Good morning Andee, is there anything important going on this morning?" Dani asked. It was a rainy Monday morning, but the weather couldn't change her happy mood.

"Good morning, no new projects so far today. Were you able to finish your last job before the wedding?" Andee Dalton asked her friend and employer.

"Thank goodness yes. It would have been a mess trying to help Paige get ready for the wedding and finish that huge project at the same time. Have you heard from the newlyweds?"

"Nah, I don't expect to. Those two are so wrapped up in each other that they don't know anyone else exists," Andee said laughing. "Hey, I wanted to ask you. I saw you reading Dain the Riot Act at the reception. What was that all about?"

"Girl, I had to stop that foolish brother of mine from pursuing Mia. You know how he gets when he has a woman in his sights." Andee nodded her agreement. "Do you know that he was on his way over to her, right after Jayden had just scattered that bunch that had surrounded her?" I wish my brother would grow up and settle down with one woman," Dani lamented.

Shaking her head, Andee commented. "You know your brother. If he has his sights on her, he's not going to stop until he gets her into his bed."

"That's what I am afraid of. I don't want to lose a friendship over his nonsense. He will only hurt Mia and then there will be a strain between Paige and Anderson and I. I just hope I got through to him." Dani was genuinely worried.

"I hear you, girl, I hear you."

"Anyway, just to reinforce my point and hopefully let him know how serious I am, I asked him to lunch today before he flies off to who knows where."

"Good luck with that one," Andee told her shaking her head, knowing that task was a lost cause.

Dain sat in his car contemplating not going inside his sister's business, *Beautiful Colors Designs*. He really didn't want to hear another lecture from his sister about his behavior or about him staying away from Mia Stone. He was a grown man who could do as he pleased. And as far as he could see, Mia was a legal adult, capable of making her own decisions, so what was the problem?

While he still planned to get Mia into bed, he found himself thinking about the other woman, the one who shot him down at the reception. Who was she and why couldn't he get her out of his head? With the way she treated him, she should be the last person on earth that he should let occupy his mind.

"She's someone I don't need to know, too much drama," he assured himself. "Besides, who needs her? There are plenty of women who won't say no." Swiping his hand down his face, Dain got out of the car to face the music.

#

"Andee, Dain should be here in a few minutes, would you send him to my office, please? Oh, and if you would like, you can join us for lunch," Dani spoke over the intercom.

Laughing Andee replied. "No thank you. I don't want to be in the middle of you two and your differences. Besides, Taylor and I have plans to have lunch together. I want to pick her brain as to where Anderson may have taken Paige for their honeymoon."

"You are so nosy," Dani replied.

Andee laughed at her response. Ending the call, she glanced in the direction of the front entrance after hearing the door swoosh close. It was Dain.

"Hey Dain, your sister is waiting for you in her office." She smiled sweetly, knowing what was coming. Back in the day when they were kids, Andee had a crush on Dain. But as time grew, with her witnessing how he treated women, Andee soon got over it. She hated the way he used his partners for his sexual gratification.

"Hello, Andee. You're looking beautiful as always. When are you going to make time for me to take you out on the town? We can have a good time just as friends, you know?" Dain asked with a grin and a wink. He already knew her answer, as per their ritual. He would ask, and she would decline with that knowing smile of hers.

Andee only grinned as she pointed towards his sister's office. He liked Andee, but always viewed her as a little sister rather than a conquest. Besides, Dani would have his head for sure if he touched any of her friends.

Just as Dain rounded the corner to join his sister in her office, the door opened again bringing Taylor inside. Taylor Patterson was Anderson and Jayden's cousin. She was Anderson's legal assistant. She and Andee had become fast friends after meeting during Paige's commission to decorate Anderson's office. Their friendship grew and solidified. Andee was just as close with Taylor as she was with Dani and Paige.

Although they were friends, Taylor remained loyal to her cousins by not divulging any personal information on the brothers, especially Jayden since Andee was dating him. Andee respected her for that but was still disappointed at not being able to learn any family secrets.

"Hey girl, you ready?" Taylor asked when she reached Andee's desk. Before she could respond, Dani and Dain rounded the corner into the reception area.

Hearing their voices, Taylor and Andee turned toward the approaching siblings.

"Oh no, not you again." Taylor's happy demeanor turned into a groan and a rolling of her eyes at the sight of a flabbergasted Dain.

Finding his voice, after his shock of seeing Taylor, Dain retorted, "Well, well, well, if it isn't the lady with the bug up her—"

"Dain! What's the matter with you?" Dani admonished her brother, horrified by his behavior towards Taylor.

"It's ok Dani. I don't expect any more from him with the way he behaved at my cousin's wedding reception. And who are you anyway?" Taylor asked with contempt dripping from her voice.

"Taylor, let me apologize for my brother. Sometimes he forgets that he was raised with manners," Dani answered for Dain, shamefully.

"Your brother?" Taylor asked, completely surprised.

"Dani, how do you know this woman?" Dain asked his sister while still eyeing the uptight Taylor.

Dani reluctantly made the introductions. "Taylor Patterson, this is my fraternal twin Dain. Dain this is Taylor, Anderson and Jayden's cousin."

"I would say it was a pleasure, but I've already been on the receiving end of your brand of *pleasure*," Taylor expressed with much sarcasm.

"Lady, I don't know what I did to upset you, but—" Dain started only to be cut off by Taylor's disbelief.

"Are you kidding me? You pompous ass!" Taylor retorted angrier than ever.

Andee, not sure what to do, during this turn of events, just sat there with her attention bouncing between Taylor and Dain as they traded insults, wondering what was going on between the two.

Recognizing that this was about to turn uglier, Dani took hold of her brother's arm and dragged him out the door, before Taylor decided to knock his block off. She could see that her brother had upset Taylor in some way and she needed to defuse the situation as soon as possible.

"Oooh, that man!." Taylor yelled with frustrated anger. "How can those two have shared the same womb? Dani is as sweet as they come, but that brother of hers is a colossal ass!" Taylor couldn't believe Dain was able to get her this riled up.

"So, I take it you two have met?" Andee commented, not knowing what to say after that exchange.

****

"Will you stop looking at that server's ass and tell me what the hell was all of that about, with Taylor?" Dani reached across the table to slap her brother's arm to get his attention. They had decided on a restaurant around the corner from Dani's office and had taken the short walk in silence.

"Ouch! That hurt!" Dain exclaimed rubbing his arm.

"Will you stop and pay attention and tell me what was that between you and Taylor, please? What did you do to her?" Dani asked, growing impatient.

"Hey, why did I have to do something? The woman could just be crazy," Dain threw back at his sister.

Dani looked at her brother doubtfully. "Uh huh, spill it!" She demanded.

Heaving a deep sigh, Dain explained the incident with Taylor during the reception. After he finished his version of the story, Dani was mortified.

"And you dare to wonder why Taylor is angry with you? Are you kidding me, Dain? You insulted that woman. You're lucky she didn't punch your freaking eyes out." Dani shook her head in disbelief.

"What? I approach all women the same way. No one has complained before," Dain whined, clearly not understanding his transgressions.

"Dain, women are not objects for you to play with whenever the mood strikes you. You know this. The problem is, too many of these women have let you get away with your behavior, be it desperation or just plain old low self-esteem. Either way, YOU know better. You have gotten so used to these foolish Pick-me's that you have forgotten what real women are like. Mom and Dad would be ashamed of your treatment of women."

Dain hated it whenever Dani brought up their parents. They had died a few years back in a car crash. Dani knew that he was still hurt over losing them so suddenly. She believed his behavior was a direct result of him not dealing with their deaths. She suggested, more than once, for him to seek therapy, but each time he declined. Dain saw nothing wrong with his lifestyle. His excuse was he always had an eye for the ladies and they for him. He just utilized that mutual attraction to his advantage, that's all.

"I think that you should go to Taylor and apologize," Dani was saying, rudely jerking him out of his musing. "Dain, are you listening to me?"

"I hear you, and not going to happen," he dismissed the suggestion.

Waitress, I'm ready to order." Dain signaled to the server, whose ass he studying earlier, firmly closing the subject of Taylor Patterson.

Dani picked up her menu shaking her head. She knew someday his behavior would bring him more trouble than he would know what to do with.

#

"So he actually did that to you?" Andee was asking Taylor after she explained why she was so angry with Dain. She wasn't surprised.

"Yes. Can you believe that guy?" Taylor asked while cutting into her steak.

Picking up her water glass, Andee took a sip before she answered Taylor's question. "Unfortunately I can. Dain has always been a little full of himself, but within the last few years, he has become the ultimate asshole. I've watched him completely degrade women with his behavior. Although not to put it all on him, the women he deals with seem to eat it up." Andee shrugged, not fully understanding herself.

"All I know is, I find the man despicable. Someone should teach him a lesson," Taylor pointed out.

"Well you know the old saying, what goes around comes around," Andee reminded. "Someday he is bound to get his."

Chapter 5

Jayden had just closed his eyes for a much-needed nap when the doorbell chimed. Opening his eyes, he cursed under his breath. He wondered who could possibly be at his door this early. He had just completed a twenty-four-hour shift and he was exhausted. He wanted to get a few hours of sleep before he had to pack and catch his flight to visit Andee. He was unable to stay in town after the wedding, because of his commitment to get back to his job, a job that he loved. Jayden was a firefighter.

Closing his eyes again, he tried to will the intruder away, but the doorbell chimed again indicating that they were not going to leave. Clad in pajama bottoms, Jayden bounded from his bed to get rid of whoever was at his door. He pulled on a tee shirt, grumbling all the way.

When he opened the door, Jayden stood staring at the grinning man who interrupted his rest. It was his estranged father, Rendell Stone.

"Hello, son."

#

Mia sat at her workstation trying to come up with a plan to land Dain Sinclair into her bed. She couldn't get him out of her thoughts. She had to have him. When it came to men, she was a connoisseur. She enjoyed the company of men as long as she was the one in control. If she saw someone she liked, she would seek him out, pretending to be the woman of his dreams, then use him, and toss him aside. She didn't see anything wrong with that, men did it all the time.

She had no desire for those emotional relationships that most women craved. Mia felt emotional attachments would only drag her down. Besides, it was much more fun this way. She could have whomever she wanted, whenever she wanted. In this respect, she was like her mother Miranda. Mia felt Miranda's only mistake was marrying her father, Rendell. Mia loved her father, but she understood Miranda.

Her mother was a beautiful woman, who embraced the value of her looks and used her beauty accordingly. Mia watched on many occasions, how men would be drawn to Miranda and how she used that attraction to garner anything that she desired. Her mother desired beautiful things, things that Rendell generously gave. However,

Miranda soon grew tired of the giver. She was never meant to belong to one man. She thrived in the variety of all the men she desired.

Mia swore that she would maintain her freedom, enjoying men as she enjoyed the delicacies at her favorite restaurant. She vowed that she would not be caught in the trap that her mother had so carelessly wandered into. A trap that Mia felt took Miranda's life too soon; torn between who she was and the woman her husband wanted her to be.

Mia settled back into her chair, mentally weaving together her plan to taste the delights of the delectable Dain Sinclair. Just the thought of him brought shivers to her body. Drawing on the information that she had collected about him, she knew just how she would accomplish her task. Sitting up in her chair, she reached for her phone to put her plan into motion.

****

Jayden didn't want to believe his father was standing in front of him, but there he was, Rendell Stone. He knew that the man existed, but to see him there in the flesh was a different matter. He hadn't known what to expect having never had the opportunity to meet the man, until now. Standing at the threshold of his home, staring at him, Jayden felt nothing. This man was a stranger in every sense of the word. He only knew of him from the stories that his mother and brother had told him over the years. He felt no connection to this outsider at all.

"Well, aren't you going to invite me in?" Rendell asked his youngest son after Jayden did not attempt to do so. Saying nothing, Jayden stepped aside to allow him to enter his home.

Jayden knew eventually, Rendell would come a calling. It was only a matter of time after he had encountered Anderson especially after he and Anderson had formed a relationship with their sister, Mia.

Rendell walked into Jayden's home looking around as he did so. He smiled as he noticed that his son had done well for himself. Jayden's furnishings were suited to him, Rendell thought. His son had good taste, just like his old man, his ego boasted. Making his way to an overstuffed sofa, Rendell made himself at home, a move that irritated Jayden. Following Rendell into his common room, he sat in a nearby chair and waited.

"Well, aren't you going to say something or ask me anything? Is there anything that you want to know?" Rendell asked his son while stretching his arms out across the back of the sofa, further irritating Jayden.

"I believe I know all there is to know about you Rendell. There isn't anything that you can tell me that I want to hear or that will change my opinion of you." Jayden's tone caused Rendell's demeanor to falter slightly.

"Although, there is one question that I would like answered. Why are you here?"

"Son, I would like to get to know you. I made some mistakes with you, your brother, and your mother. I would like to make amends for leaving you all those years ago," Rendell explained, hoping to make some progress with him.

Here was this man, his so-called father looking for forgiveness. Jayden stared at a stranger who gave him life but didn't stick around to nurture it. His mother and brother had done that. He couldn't decide if it was because of lack of sleep or if he genuinely felt nothing for him. Whatever the reason, Jayden knew he didn't want anything to do with Rendell Stone.

Rendell—" Jayden started only to be cut off by this interloper.

"I'm your father, son," Rendell arrogantly corrected.

"Rendell," Jayden repeated, ignoring him. "I don't know you nor do I want to know you. I am too old to need a daddy and since you didn't stick around to become one, I don't see the point in you starting now. Oh and one more thing, don't call me son. Only men who are fathers get to use that term. So if there isn't anything else, I would like to get back to my nap that you so rudely interrupted." Jayden spoke to Rendell in a cold, harsh tone, fully expecting his so-called father to get the message.

Sitting forward from his relaxed position, Rendell replied, "Look son...ur...Jayden," Rendell quickly corrected, not wanting to press his luck before voicing what he came there to say.

"How long are you all going to punish me for my past mistakes? I told your mother and brother that I was sorry. Why isn't that enough for you?" Rendell asked him frustrated.

"What the hell do you mean you told my mother? Have you been bothering her?" At the mere mention of his mother, Jayden jumped to his feet; fully intent on pounding this stranger into the ground.

When Jayden lunged at him, Rendell tried to move quickly from his seat on the sofa, but Jayden was quicker. Catching him by his collar, Jayden dog-walked him towards the door.

"You stay away from my mother old man, or so help me I will make you pay!" Wanting very much to hit Rendell, but fighting hard against it, Jayden dragged him through the front door and shoved him out onto the porch, slamming the door behind him.

#

Dain sat in the cockpit preparing for a short round-trip flight to Omaha. While checking his gauges and overhead panels, he thought about his conversation with Dani to apologize to Taylor. Why should he? There were far too many women out there to worry about one. Besides, he doubted that he would ever see her again. It wasn't as if he would seek her out for anything. Why would he? She made it quite clear that she had no use for him. Besides, he liked his women compliant. The less fuss the better.

Still, the woman captivated him. He had never come across a woman who rejected his charms. Women usually swarmed him like metal to a magnet. This woman did not. But why does his mind keep returning to the night of the reception? He remembered what drew his attention to her. Taylor was tall and shapely. She had a body that men got excited over, with her full breasts, narrow waist, and rounded hips. He liked all sizes of women from the size two ladies to the tall full-figured girls. As long as they were beautiful and legal, he was happy to take them to on.

Still, he questioned himself. He was happy—right? Dain began to question his methods in his treatment of women. Taylor's reaction nagged at him. Was he indeed over the top with his behavior? It wasn't as if he were putting a gun to women's heads to force them into bed with him. It was their choice. What's more, they got just as much pleasure out of the encounters as he did. Didn't they?

Dain shook his head. He was overthinking things. He had to get Taylor Patterson out of his head. She had no right to be there questioning his life. Pushing those thoughts from his mind, Dain pulled his attention back to the task at hand. Receiving clearance from the tower, he and his crew prepared for flight.

#

After his return flight back to Metro City, Rendell drove quickly back to his hotel. He let himself into his suite, still visibly shaken by Jayden's behavior. He couldn't believe it. His son had wanted to physically hurt him. The rage he saw in Jayden's eyes scared him. Jayden's reaction was much more than his brother's when he and Mia had happened to run into him in a restaurant months ago. With Anderson, he felt his anger much more than saw it. Rendell couldn't understand how Jayden could have so much more rage against a man he never met before today.

Taking a healthy swallow from the drink that he had poured for himself, his hands shook as he recalled the naked fury in Jayden's eyes. Rendell shuddered. Jayden was his last hope of ever getting his family back and he had failed. It was all over now. Both of his sons despised him and his ex-wife loathed him. There was nothing he could do but accept the facts.

Rendall took another swallow from his glass just as someone knocked on the door. It was Mia. She took one look at her father and hugged him.

"I have really messed things up, Mia. There is no way that I can make amends for my sins now," he told his daughter.

He had called Mia as soon as he landed, asking her to meet him back at his hotel. There was no one else to call. She had rushed right over, after hearing the emotional defeat in her father's voice.

"Papa maybe if you could just give them a little more time. They will come around, you'll see," Mia pleaded with him. She had never seen him like this before. He sat in the wing-backed chair appearing small and frail. Mia had always known her father to be full of life, full of energy, nothing like this. She began to resent her brothers for putting their father through this. Sure Rendell made some mistakes in the past, but he had owned up to those mistakes and was willing to set things right. Why couldn't his sons see that?

Sitting there watching her father retreat inside himself, Mia grew angry towards Jayden and Anderson.

Why wouldn't they just give him a chance? Rendell deserved a second chance. Mia loved her father unconditionally. She never saw the smug arrogant side of him that her brothers and Adaisha had witnessed. He was her father. The man who raised her with as much love and caring as any father could have. She could have understood had he not been remorseful, wanting only what was best for himself. Rendell loved all of his children and wanted to show that love to Anderson and Jayden.

"Papa, why don't you go lie down for a while? I'm sure you will feel better once you've rested," she coaxed.

Mia helped him up and into the bedroom. After she had gotten him settled, she let herself out. She felt that she had to do something to help her father. She would talk to her brothers again concerning their relationship with him. They had to give him a second chance; they just had to.

Taylor stared at Mia as she ranted about needing to speak to Anderson. She couldn't believe the nerve of this woman-child as she stood there at her desk, demanding to know the whereabouts of her honeymooning boss. Taylor had been given strict instructions not to divulge their location unless it was a life-or-death emergency. Listening to this girl talk about her father's need to be a part of his sons' lives did not come close. She let her talk a few moments more before she shut her down in mid-rant.

"Mia, your need to speak with your brother will have to wait until he returns from his honeymoon. You know the time that one spends with one's new spouse after exchanging vows at the altar," Taylor reminded her sarcastically. "Your request is not an emergency so it will have to wait, and that's final."

Taylor punctuated this last statement by turning back to her computer screen. She had only come into the office to receive some documents that were to be delivered, while Anderson was away.

"Well, when does he come back?" Mia asked her impatiently. She wanted to give Anderson a piece of her mind about Rendell. She had called Jayden about his part in upsetting their father, but she had gotten his voicemail. So Anderson was the next best thing until she had forgotten he was out of town.

"He will be back in a few days. He didn't give a precise date. I am sure he will contact you when he and

Paige get home." Taylor was growing impatient with this spoiled diva. She recognized Mia wasn't used to being told no. Too bad Taylor thought with a small smile.

Dismissing Taylor with a flip of her long wavy hair, Mia turned to leave the office without so much as a goodbye. Rolling her eyes, Taylor continued with her task.

Chapter 6

"I didn't tell you that Rendell had visited me because I knew that it would upset you," Adaisha was explaining to her youngest son.

After Jayden had thrown his father out of his house, he called his mother to confront her about Rendell's visit. After not getting an answer on either of her phones, he was headed to her house, for fear Rendell had made a second surprise visit that day. Just as he opened his door to leave, he found Adaisha, poised to ring the doorbell.

"No Mom you should have told us. Anderson and I had a right to know that he has been harassing you. We don't know what that man is capable of." Jayden was furious with his mother for not sharing Rendell's late-night visit with him and Anderson.

"Son, had I known that he would come to you with his nonsense, I would have told you. Besides, it was just that one visit," Adaisha assured with a weary sigh. She couldn't believe the depths that man would go to insinuate himself into their lives. How many times and how many ways can they rebuff him before he gives up?

"Mom, please promise me that you will let me know the next time he shows up because he will try you again. He seems that determined," Jayden predicted.

"Ok, ok I promise. But you don't have to worry about me, Matthew is always around. He can and will look after me," Adaisha reminded him.

"Where was Matthew the night Rendell showed up?" Jayden asked with a raised brow.

"He was out of town on business, but I have discussed this with him so you don't have to worry," Adaisha quickly informed him. "I thought you had to pack for your visit to Andee's?" She asked, trying to change the subject.

Looking at his watch, Jayden responded. "I have time. I just want to make sure that you're ok. That man has no right to be bothering you under any circumstances. You owe him nothing!"

"Jayden I'm fine," she assured him, patting his hand. "As I told you before, Rendell has no more power over me. Besides, after his last visit to my home, I doubt if he will be bothering me again."

Although not convinced, Jayden dropped the subject of Rendell. "Mom, you haven't told me why you've come by."

"Oh yes, I almost forgot. Your brother and Paige are due back in a couple of days and Dani has planned a small welcome home reception at her home. She would like the family to be there. How long will you be visiting Andee?"

"I planned to be there for a few days so I will be there for the party. You did say that it will be just the family right?" He asked her, not wanting a repeat performance with his sister and those hounds that were sniffing around her at the wedding reception.

"Yes, just the family and a few friends. Matthew will be joining me on this trip as well. He hated that he missed the wedding."

"Well good mom, I'm glad you have Matthew in your life. As long as he makes you happy, I'm happy." Jayden kissed his mother's cheek.

Adaisha was glad to hear it. She knew that her boys didn't have a problem with her dating Matthew, but she wondered how they would react when they discovered they were married. Oh well, she thought, she would know soon enough because they planned to announce their marriage at the dinner party.

Chapter 7

Having plotted out her plan carefully, Mia waited her turn to board the plane headed to New York City. She appeared calm, but she was anything but. She was anxious for what was sure to come. After calling in favors, and obtaining information she needed concerning which flight Dain would be flying that day, Mia put her plan into action.

"Good morning, nice to have you aboard." She heard the pilot of the huge jet aircraft greet his passengers as they came aboard the plane. She was several commuters back, watching as he smiled at everyone who passed him.

"Well hello, it's nice to have you flying with us today," a surprised Dain greeted Mia when it was her turn to board the plane.

Taking her hand, he assisted her across the threshold. Dain had saved his widest and brightest smile that morning, for this unexpected passenger. Realizing that he was preventing the others from boarding, he reluctantly let go of Mia's hand, but not before, he had made it clear, that he would be seeing her after they landed.

On landing at LaGuardia, Mia made it a point to be the last person to exit the plane. She took her time approaching the exit, and as expected, Dain was waiting for her. Extending his hand to her as she approached him, he made his pitch.

"I hope your flight was enjoyable."

Mia nodded and smiled, demurely. Belying what she had in store for this gorgeous man.

"As you may have guessed, I was your Captain during this flight, but I would like to formally introduce myself, Dain Sinclair." Dain offered his hand to Mia.

"I believe you attended Paige and Anderson's wedding. I tried making it a priority to introduce myself then, but your brother had other ideas," Dain continued with a grin that was not quite lecherous, but close.

Accepting his hand Mia responded. "Mia Stone...and I apologize for my overprotective brother. He can be a bit much sometimes," she explained, giving Dain her sexiest smile.

"Well, I hope that we can get to know each other while you're in town. I don't have to be back in the air for a

few days. Will your stay here be business or pleasure?"
Dain asked Mia, hoping that her trip would be all his
pleasure.

"Actually, I'm here on a mini vacation. I thought
that I would come to the Big Apple and do a little
sightseeing, some shopping…"

"…And having room service with me," Dain
finished her sentence for her. Still smiling, he took her hand
and escorted her from the plane.

#

Dain and Mia took a taxi to an upscale hotel that
was far enough away from the prying eyes of his
crewmembers and hopefully from anyone else who may
know his sister or her brother. Mia lounged in the lobby
while Dain checked them in, excited by the upcoming
events.

Joining some of the other guests of the hotel, they
rode the elevator to the seventeenth floor in silence. Each
contemplated what would happen once they closed the door
to their rented room. They didn't have long to wait. As
soon as Dain opened the door to the expensive suite, Mia
pushed him inside, dropped her carry-on, and shoved him

up against the nearest wall. They kissed and fondled each other with a hunger that had been building since the flight.

Mia nearly tore Dain out of his jacket, as she attempted to disrobe him in one fell swoop. Matching her urgency, he took over, removing his clothes quickly. After discarding his, he stripped Mia of hers. Guiding him to the bed, Mia pushed him onto it, climbing on top of him. Dain was in heaven. Here was this beautiful woman straddling him and she was his for the taking.

Lying there, he took note of her beautifully sculpted body. Her skin was smooth and taunt. Her exotic features complemented her olive-toned skin. Her hair full, silky, and long, teased his chest as she proceeded to kiss his body, moving south with each kiss of her lips. At each delicate trace of those beautiful lips, Dain grew harder anticipating the results, once her mouth reached him.

However, as Mia drew closer to her goal, without warning, Taylor's seductive face popped into his mind. Startled, Dain's eyes widened as he envisioned Taylor's pouting mouth kissing his body instead of Mia's. Not knowing what to make of this, but feeling disturbed, Dain shook his head to rid himself of this vision. Needing to free himself of Taylor casually lounging in his mind, he didn't wait for Mia to reach her target.

Grabbing her by her narrow waist, he flipped her onto her back. Taking only a few experienced seconds to protect himself, Dain closed his eyes and plunged deep inside of her. He rode her fiercely, trying to hammer Taylor from his mind. However, when he opened them to enjoy the expression on Mia's pleasure-riddled face, what he saw was Taylor's beautifully sated features. Wanting to end this madness, Dain turned Mia over onto her stomach, entering her from behind. This time he continued his pleasure with Mia, and only Mia with each stroke.

#

Having accomplished her goal, Mia sat in her assigned seat and headed home, fully satisfied. She and Dain had spent the last two days in bed mating like rabbits. She knew that he would be good, but she was unprepared for the sensations that he brought out in her. He was by far the best lover she had encountered. Mia was certain that no one could top him. She ranked him high enough for her to consider breaking her own rule of no engagement. She needed to have more of him. She wanted to have all of him.

Settling back into her first-class seat, Mia made plans to make Dain Sinclair a permanent part of her life.

#

Dain let himself into his house exhausted. He had just completed a very long flight. Usually, he wasn't this tired, but after spending two days in bed with an insatiable Mia, he was drained. He found her to be an incredible woman, but all the same just another woman. He did not intend to see her again.

Stopping long enough to relieve himself of his shoes, he tiredly lumbered over to the counter that divided the common area from the kitchen, to retrieve his mail. Whenever he was away his sister would drop in to water the plants and check on the place.

There were several pieces of mail, none important. Tossing the pile back onto the counter, yawning, he drowsily moved on to the refrigerator for a beer. Attached to the door was a note from Dani informing him that she was hosting a small dinner party for the newlyweds on their return home. She also informed him that she fully expected him to be there and on his best behavior.

After reading the note, he tossed it in the trash. He didn't plan to attend, especially if Mia would be there. While he had enjoyed her, she was not to be repeated. On their last day together, he recognized the look that women got when they wanted more than sex from him. He couldn't risk seeing her again. On the other hand, he wondered if Taylor would be there.

Over the two days that he spent with Mia, Taylor had shown herself in his fantasies more times than he could count. She was the reason he was more amorously aggressive with Mia than he had planned to be. He was trying to exorcise her from his thoughts.

What was it about that woman? She had shot him down and made him question himself and his actions. He didn't like that. However, at the same time, he couldn't get her out of his head. No, he wouldn't go to the party. He didn't need to see either of those women again. With this settled, Dain decided against the beer and continued into his bedroom, before collapsing onto the bed, falling asleep immediately.

Chapter 8

Jayden watched Anderson's jaw tighten. "Hey I know that look bro, so whatever you're planning, include me. It took everything in me not to break that old man's face. I couldn't believe that he had the balls to show up at mom's like that."

Anderson was livid. Jayden had just filled him in on what Rendell had been up to, while he was away on his honeymoon. It was bad enough that Rendell had found his way to Jayden's, but to bother their mother was intolerable. As soon as he was able to find some time, Anderson planned to track Rendell down and make sure he understood he was not to go anywhere near their mother, ever. He was going to make sure Rendell would never hurt Adaisha again.

"Hey you two, why the serious faces?" Paige asked her husband and brother-in-law. "You two have been huddled over here since Andee and Jayden arrived."

"We're fine babe. Jayden was just filling me in on some of our male guests who were getting too cozy with Mia at the reception." Not wanting to alarm his wife,

Anderson hugged and kissed her, reassuring her there wasn't a problem.

Anderson eyed his brother above Paige's head, silently swearing him to secrecy. Understanding fully, Jayden nodded slightly.

Rolling her eyes at Jayden's bullying antics, Paige turned to him. "You have to stop playing the big bully when it comes to your sister Jayden. She is a grown woman capable of handling herself. And who's to say that she doesn't like the attention? Have you tried asking her that?" She asked him.

It was Jayden's turn to roll his eyes because he believed Mia to be an innocent young woman. She didn't know how badly men could treat women. He wanted to protect her from the ways of the world.

"Did I hear someone call my name?" Mia asked as she joined her brothers and new sister-in-law. "Welcome home you two," She added, hugging Paige and then Anderson. "Paige, may I have a moment with my brothers please?" Mia asked sweetly. Although she had time to cool off over her brothers' rejection of Rendell, she still planned to give them both a piece of her mind.

"I want to talk to you both about our father," she started the moment Paige stepped away. She was prepared to tear into them when Anderson stopped her.

"Mia, we will not discuss this here tonight. Taylor told me about your little visit to my office the other day, ranting about Rendell. If you want to discuss this further you can meet with me and Jayden at my house tomorrow. Ok?" Mia nodded. Glancing at Jayden, Anderson knew the hard-packed feelings he and his brother had against Rendell were not going to change. Mia would just have to accept that fact.

#

Dain slipped into his sister's home unnoticed. He didn't know why he was there. He had told Dani that he had to work and would not be in attendance at the party. But here he was, pacing in his sister's kitchen, trying to decide if he had made the right decision. He told himself that he was there because he didn't want to let his sister down when in reality he was there to see Taylor. The woman haunted his dreams. The more he tried to forget her the more she seemed to dig deeper inside him.

Suddenly feeling that he may have made a mistake in coming there, Dain turned to leave only to have his sister come into the room.

"Dain, I thought you couldn't make it...never mind. I'm glad that you're here. Come on, everyone is in the other room." Dani took hold of her brother's arm and dragged him into the living room. "Look who I found," Dani announced to her guests.

Dain groaned inwardly. As soon as he entered the room he locked eyes with Mia. He was so intent on seeing Taylor, that he had forgotten his resolve to stay away from Mia. From the determined look on her face, he immediately knew he had made a mistake, and to top it off Taylor wasn't even there.

"Hello everyone," he half-heartedly spoke to the room, trying to sound cheery, but feeling anything but. Everyone said their hellos as he toured the room, trying to stay as far away from Mia as he could.

Dani, watching the interaction or the lack of interaction between her brother and Mia, silently groaned. She could tell from the radiant look plastered on Mia's face and the expression of unease on Dain's that they had slept together, which meant Dain was done with her. Dani was angry with her brother, but it would have to wait until later, for she had guests to entertain.

"So Anderson and Paige, are you two ready to tell us where you went for your honeymoon?" Matthew was asking the happy couple. "And by the way, I want to apologize again for not being able to attend the wedding. You know how long those overseas flights are," he added.

"Matthew, not a problem. We're glad that you were able to be with us tonight," Anderson assured him. "And to answer your question, I took my lovely bride to Paris for our honeymoon. It was a city that was on her wish list of places to visit, so I surprised her by making that wish come true." Anderson turned to his beaming wife, kissing her affectionately.

"Wow…What a beautiful city to honeymoon in. Although I've only seen photos, I hear the city is gorgeous, especially at night," Andee commented, as the room erupted with excitement over the couple's trip.

"I've visited the city many times," Dain chimed in. "It's a beautiful city for lovers, for sure," he added without thinking.

He immediately regretted the statement, after witnessing Mia's knowing grin. Groaning again, he was now certain that it was a mistake to have come there.

As everyone gathered around them, Paige and Anderson proceeded to tell the group about their trip, sharing photos and souvenirs they had brought back for everyone. While most of the group was concentrating on the couple's blissful moments in Paris, Mia had made her way across the room to Dain. She was on him before he could react.

"Hi lover, I was beginning to think you wouldn't make it to the party," she crooned seductively.

"Will you keep your voice down? You know how your brother is," Dain whispered, with eyes darting around the room and trying not to appear guilty.

"Oops, sorry. When can I see you again?" She asked him, hoping that they could hook up later that night.

"Mia, —"

"Dain, can you help me with the food in the kitchen?" Dani asked her brother sweetly. She had been monitoring the situation from across the room and had quickly moved in to prevent a scene. She knew when her brother was about to dump someone. She had witnessed this scenario too many times before. Dani did not want her dinner party ruined by shouting and crying, which was sure to follow.

Relieved that Dani had swooped in, Dain thankfully followed her into the kitchen. He knew it was the wrong time and place to give his usual "it was fun, but" speech, however, he needed to nip the Mia situation in the bud as soon as possible. He should have listened to Dani and stayed away from her. He just hoped that Taylor never found out about it.

Taylor? Where did that come from? The concept alarmed him. Why should he care what she thought? She wasn't anything to him. He didn't even like the woman. Before he could begin to dissect this thought further, Dani smacked him on the back of his head.

"What the hell were you thinking Dain? You slept with that girl after I specifically told you to stay away…really? She whispered through clenched teeth. "Unbelievable!" Throwing up her hands, Dani paced the floor, furious with her brother.

Coming to a sudden stop, she glanced around him to make sure they weren't being overheard, then continued. "Why Dain, why couldn't you leave her alone? If those people out there take one look at that girl, they will know something is up and start asking questions. And you better hope like hell she doesn't spill the beans because Jayden will definitely beat the shit out of you and I just might let him."

Not really having an answer that would please her, Dain remained mute. Dani was right, he didn't think, at least not with the correct head anyway. For the first time in his life, Dain Sinclair felt remorse. Although he didn't regret sleeping with Mia, he was fearful that someone might find out, someone like Taylor. He didn't know why it was important to him that she not discover this bit of information, he just knew that it was.

"One thing is for sure…" Dani was saying, "…you will not dump that girl tonight and not here. Do you understand me? This is a joyous occasion and it will remain one. So grab those oven mitts and help me serve this food." Having diverted the disaster of the decade, Dani stepped away from him to continue her hosting duties.

Dain could only comply with his sister's wishes. He knew that she was right. He couldn't break it off with Mia there and certainly not now. Jayden, if not Anderson, would beat him to a bloody pulp, then Taylor was sure to find out. One thing was clear, he knew he had to leave soon to explore the obsession he had with a woman he wasn't even certain he liked. He needed to understand why she mattered.

The rest of the evening went as planned. The families and friends enjoyed the food, drink, and ambiance that Dani had created for them. Whenever Dani noticed that Mia was getting too close to her brother she ran interference, keeping them apart the entire night. It was a miracle that no one else noticed the huge elephant in the room. As the party started to wind down, Matthew tapped his glass with a spoon to get everyone's attention.

"Excuse me, excuse me, everyone. I would like to make an announcement before everyone heads out." Taking his wife's hand, he cleared his throat. "A few weeks ago this lovely lady made me the happiest man on earth…well besides you Anderson," he conceded with a chuckle. "Adaisha has made me happy by becoming my wife."

The room exploded with surprise and congratulations. Anderson and Jayden hugged and kissed their mother and shook hands with Matthew, giving them both their blessings. While the room was busy congratulating the happy couple, Dain saw his chance to leave unnoticed by Mia and his sister.

Letting himself out the backdoor, he made his way around to the front of Dani's house. As he walked towards his car, he spotted someone coming up the walkway. It was Taylor, and he was overjoyed to see her.

#

Mia looked around for Dain. Not finding him inside, she discreetly made her way outside to search for him. As she stepped out into the yard, she spotted him pulling a reluctant Taylor down the street to his car. She watched while he held the door for her as she settled herself in the passenger seat. She watched as they drove away.

Mia was furious. Why was he with her? Why had Taylor left with him? She didn't even like him. Mia planned to get to the bottom of this. She would not allow another woman to come between her and Dain.

Chapter 9

Not wasting any time, Dain grabbed Taylor by the arm; trying to hurry her to his car.

"Hey, what are you doing?" Taylor asked him protesting all the way.

"Just come with me, I will explain later." Sensing that she was about to protest again, and loudly, he added, "Please." He didn't want to alert the guests inside, especially not Mia.

Once they were inside his car and he had pulled away from the curb, heading out of the subdivision, Dain spoke. "Where did you park your car?" He asked her.

"I had to park almost a block away because of all the other cars, …Dain, what is this all about?" She asked him again.

Relieved that she'd parked far enough away that no one would know she had been there, Dain tried to explain. "Taylor, I…"

What was he going to say? That he couldn't stop thinking about her and it had nothing to do with sex. How could he say that without sounding…what? He didn't know. All he did know was that he felt great joy when he saw her heading towards him. He needed her, he just didn't know how or why. Unable to say any of those things, Dain said the one thing he thought he would never say to a woman.

"Taylor, I'm sorry for my behavior towards you at the wedding reception. I was out of line and I hope that you will forgive me." There, he said it. Now what?

#

After driving for a while with Taylor not saying a word, Dain brought them to a coffee shop where they sat in silence, both unsure of what to say next. Dain was nervous because Taylor hadn't addressed his apology and he wanted, no, needed her to forgive him. He sat there holding the warm coffee mug between his palms, waiting for her to say something, anything. After a long moment, she finally spoke.

"I believe that you are sincere Dain," Taylor addressed him. Noticing the puzzled look on his face, she clarified her statement. "Your apology, I believe that you are sincere. And the reason that I believe you is because, since we have come into this coffee shop, several women have tried to get your attention and you have ignored them all. Not one time did you look at their breasts or behinds. I'm impressed," she finished with a small smile.

Dain lowered his hunched shoulders with relief. That was one hurdle that he had gotten over. Could he manage the others? He briefly glanced around the shop, at the women that Taylor had mentioned and indeed, they were all clamoring for his attention. Dain turned back to Taylor, dismissing them immediately. He was so bent on her approval, that he didn't care who was there.

Taylor studied him. He seemed subdued, almost human she thought. She wondered what brought about this change in him because the man she had encountered previously would have never apologized for his actions.

Finally finding his voice, Dain spoke. "So does this mean that you accept my apology?" He asked.

Chapter 10

Relieved that the night was over without any mishaps, Dani was grateful despite that one moment of panic. During Matthew's announcement, she had taken her eyes off Dain and Mia for a second, only to find that they both had disappeared. She almost lost it. She was sure that her brother was outside with Mia giving her the boot. But to her relief, Mia returned without a tear shed. Dani didn't know what happened, but she was just grateful it wasn't explosive.

"So, you want to tell me what all that was about earlier?" Devin asked Dani after the guests had left and they were in the kitchen cleaning up.

"What was what all about?" She asked clearly puzzled by his question.

"Dani I watched you play out a little drama with your brother here in this kitchen earlier, then there was the Mia blocking the rest of the night. What was going on?"

Dani groaned and dropped her head. She was unaware that anyone had noticed the undercurrent of foolishness that had played out during the party. After learning that Devin had witnessed the entire mess, she wondered who else had noticed. She was just delighted that neither Jayden nor Anderson had caught on.

"The short version is Dain slept with Mia and had tried to dump her during the party. That was before I put a stop to it. Can you imagine the carnage that would have taken place had he dumped that girl in the middle of my dinner party? I had warned Dain at the reception to stay away from her, but nooo, he had to have her, and now there is this huge mess."

Shaking his head, Devin understood. "That brother of yours is going to dig himself into a hole he won't be able to dig himself out of. And just to give you a heads up, I wasn't the only one who saw what was happening between you three. Andee picked up on it and asked me what was going on. So expect her questions about it tomorrow." Devin leaned over and gave her a comforting kiss before continuing his task of stacking dishes into the dishwasher.

How was she going to keep that particular cat in the bag if Andee knew? She just hoped that she could head her off before she said something to Jayden. Thinking that this couldn't wait until tomorrow, Dani reached for the phone to call her.

****

"Girl I might be nosy but I am not crazy," Andee was telling Dani.

They discussed the Mia and Dain situation in the office. Paige was technically still on her honeymoon, so they were free to speak without being overheard.

"Andee I couldn't sleep not knowing what you may have said to Jayden. I almost drove over to your place after I couldn't get you on the phone, but you have to thank Devin for stopping me," she added laughing.

"Well had you shown up at my place, you would have surely gotten drama if you had interrupted Jayden's mission. And believe me, the drama would not have come from Jayden. Andee told her laughing.

"Seriously though, I would never tell Jayden about Dain and his sister. I am all for keeping the peace. Besides Mia is a grown woman so he has no right to behave as if she were a child. I have tried to reason with him but he won't budge. How do you think Anderson would feel about the situation?"

"How would I feel about what situation," he asked suddenly. Dani and Andee turned startled. They hadn't heard him enter the office. His gaze swung from one woman to the other.

Dani took the lead, attempting to clean it up the best way she could. "We were just discussing…"

"Your brother sleeping with my sister? I know all about that," he stated. Both women stood there with their mouths ajar.

"Don't look so stunned. I think everyone at the party last night knew what was going on, with the exception of my brother. And if Jayden would take the blinders off and stop viewing Mia as some innocent child, he would have been aware of it too."

"So how do you feel about it?" Andee asked.

"Well, I don't like it. Considering, Dani, that your brother is a degenerate womanizer and all…no offense…

"None taken," Dani answered.

"…but those two are consenting adults and it is not my place to stick my nose in grown folk's business. I certainly wouldn't want anyone sticking their nose in mine and Paige's bedroom," he added with a shrug. "And if it comes up with Jayden, I will make it a point to remind him of that. But in the meantime, I would suggest that your brother lay low, so he doesn't find out."

Dani nodded. "I'll do my best to make that happen," she assured him.

"Oh, the reason that I'm here," Anderson snapped his fingers. "Paige sent me after some paperwork that she needs to work on at home. Can you ladies help me find it?"

Chapter 11

Dain whistled a tune as he let himself into his home. He had just gotten in from his London flight and looked forward to having a cold beer and a hot shower. The trip had been uneventful, with no turbulence or storms, which made his job easier. Closing the door that led to the garage, he headed for the kitchen, only to be stopped short by a noise coming from his bedroom. Retracing his steps, Dain made his way to a hidden drawer where he kept a handgun.

Retrieving the weapon, he quietly made his way to his bedroom. Adrenalin pumping, he tried to recall if Dani had mentioned she would be dropping by. She often did when he was out of town. No that couldn't be right, her car would have been parked in his driveway had she been here, he thought. This was definitely an intruder.

Slowly he opened the bedroom door, prepared to confront the trespasser. Hearing the noise again, he pushed the door open with force, leveling the gun at the person who dared enter his home.

"Hello lover, I don't think you will be needing that." Mia greeted him fully nude and stretched out across his bed. "At least you won't need that type of gun anyway," she added, smiling seductively.

"Mia, what the hell are doing here?" He asked, lowering the gun but completely annoyed. "And how did you get into my house, not to mention know where I live?"

"To answer your first question, since you wouldn't return my calls I thought that I would surprise you with a welcome home gift. You like?" She asked while spreading her legs.

Dain closed his eyes, not believing this was happening. He had ignored calls and messages he had received from her, hoping that she would get the hint. However, here she was bare ass naked on his bed.

Shoving the gun into his waistband, Dain leaned against the doorjamb. "Mia, how do you know where I live? I never told you *or* invited you for that matter."

"Well, I have my ways," she told him.

Her way was following him from the airport one night after one of his flights. She tried to obtain the information from his sister but she wouldn't tell her, so she had to use other means. She should have known Dani wouldn't give her the information, considering she had kept them apart all evening during the dinner party. She suspected that Dani didn't like her.

"Whatever your means are, you had no right to come to my home unannounced or uninvited." Dain was becoming more irritated by the minute. He was incensed that she was there. Suppose he had brought a woman back to his place, he thought, although that was highly unlikely. Nevertheless, he could have brought Taylor home with him.

Ah, Taylor. She had forgiven him and he was grateful. They had sat in that coffee shop, until the wee hours of the morning just talking, something he never bothered to do with any other woman. He found that he enjoyed just sitting there with her, sharing over cups of coffee. He had found her interesting and exciting. For the first time in his life, Dain was interested in a woman and it had nothing to do with her body or him trying to get her into his bed. He genuinely liked Taylor and hoped to see her again. She was still a little hesitant about him but promised to keep an open mind. That was all that he could ask for, considering the way he had treated her when they first met. He planned to prove to her that he could be a better man and that he could be a friend, which is all that she would allow him to be under the circumstances. And he couldn't blame her.

Yet here was Mia Stone, a problem that he had created by sleeping with her. A problem that could jeopardize his progress with Taylor, if he didn't put a stop to her nonsense and quickly.

"Mia, you need to get dressed. We had a good time in New York, but it was nothing more than that. You know that I am not the committing type. We discussed that from the beginning. You are a great girl, but you should find someone willing to be there for you in the long run. I'm not that man, so please get up, get dressed, and leave."

Not giving her a chance to respond, Dain turned on his heels and left the room to give her some privacy. He retraced his steps back to the kitchen for that much-needed beer.

A few minutes later, Mia emerged from the bedroom fully clothed. He could tell that she had been crying, by the way that she sniffled and by the avoidance of eye contact. He hated to have to be so blunt, but he never beat around the bush when it came to the women he entertained. He learned early on that not setting clear boundaries could cause trouble later.

"I won't bother you again," Mia was saying as she hurried to the door to let herself out.

She couldn't believe he rejected her. There she was displayed for the taking and he just ignored her, dumped her. Sure, they had discussed the terms of their hookup on the ride to the hotel in New York. It was understood there would be no strings attached, and she had agreed. But that was before she knew how good he was.

Mia needed a man like Dain. He was handsome, intelligent, and heaven, when it came to the bedroom. She had never encountered a lover like Dain, one who knew ways to please a woman that she hadn't known existed let alone experienced.

She wondered if Taylor had anything to do with his change in attitude. She would leave for now, but she was determined to get him to understand that they were meant to be together. Mia vowed that Dain Sinclair would be hers.

Chapter 12

Taylor sat at her desk replaying her evening with
Dain. She didn't know what to make of him. They had sat
in that coffee shop enjoying each other's company,
something she didn't think Dain was capable of doing. She
felt that he was sincere in his apology; she just couldn't
pinpoint what had brought about the sudden change in him.
He was a very interesting man, once you got past the
pompous-ass mode that he was usually locked into.

She learned he was an airline pilot who loved his
job and took it very seriously. He explained witnessing
fellow pilots ruin their careers, by drinking or napping on
the job. He made it clear that when he was in the air, with
passengers who trusted him, he followed protocol to the
letter. He never took lightly the lives that he was
responsible for. She wondered how a man so passionate
about his work could be so callous when it came to women.
She shook her head. The man was an enigma.

Listening to him talk about his job, and the love he
had for his sister and deceased parents, Taylor saw the
human, softer side of Dain. She felt he wasn't all bad, but
just had lost his way. Even though she did warm up to him,

she was still smarting from the behavior that he displayed the first time she had encountered him. She let him know that although she had forgiven him, it didn't mean that she had let her guard down. She still felt that despicable person still resided inside him.

After bringing her back to her car that night, she sensed that he was reluctant to let her leave. Each time she had attempted to exit his car, he asked her more questions about her life, her hopes and dreams. This truly puzzled her, because men like Dain Sinclair could care less about a woman's dreams. Yes, Mr. Sinclair had her truly perplexed.

"Hi, Taylor. How was your time off?" Anderson asked. Anderson had taken an extra week to spend with his new wife before resuming business, giving Taylor an extra week of leave.

"It was enjoyable, but not as fun as you're honeymoon I'll bet. Oh and Anderson, I'm sorry that I didn't make it to Dani's dinner party. How was it?" she asked.

"It was great. Paige and I had a good time. And, don't worry about missing it, I'm sure that whatever kept you away was well worth it," he told her while he sifted through the messages that she handed him.

Although she did spend a surprisingly pleasant evening with a man whom she thought was a total idiot, she was still undecided if it was worth it. Anderson spoke again, bringing her out of her musing.

"Jayden told me you encountered some idiot at our reception that made you uncomfortable. Are you ok?" Anderson asked her concerned.

"Oh, it was nothing." Taylor waved it off. "Just a partier that had a little too much to drink is all. I handled him. I think that you would have been proud of me," she chuckled, not wanting to tell him that the idiot was Dain Sinclair.

"Well ok, but if he bothers you again let me know and we can get a restraining order issued," Anderson assured her.

Taylor only nodded. She wasn't about to tell her cousin that not only had she forgiven the man, but she had accepted a dinner invitation from him for later in the week. She still didn't know what made her accept.

The last attempt she had made to get out of his car, Dain blurted out that he would like to see her again. He made it plain that it was just dinner, nothing more, and that he would be a complete gentleman the entire time. Not thinking, she had accepted, which seemed to have pleased them both, a reaction that she continued to ponder, especially on her part.

#

Coming to the end of a full workday, Taylor said good night to Anderson and rode the elevator down to the parking garage. Searching in her purse for her keys, she didn't notice the broken windows until glass crunched under her feet when she reached her car. Surprised colored her face before fear settled in, causing her to retreat into the elevator and then into Anderson's office.

Taylor startled Anderson by bursting through his door, bringing him quickly to his feet. "Taylor, what's wrong?" He asked her, troubled by the fear in her eyes.

"Some…someone broke out all of my car windows Anderson, every last one of them," she stammered.

Alarmed, Anderson told her to stay put while he went to investigate.

Reaching the garage, he indeed found that all of Taylor's windows had been smashed including the windshield and back window. He immediately called building security and the police.

After the police had taken their statements and security had promised to keep a closer look out, Anderson questioned Taylor.

"I know you told the police that you didn't know who could have done this, but it's me, Taylor, you can tell me?" Anderson coaxed her.

Shaking her head, Taylor reiterated what she told the police. "Honestly Anderson, I don't know anyone who would do such a thing to me. As far as I know, I don't have any enemies."

"What about that guy from the wedding reception, could he have done this?" He asked her, quickly placing the mystery man at the top of his list of suspects.

"No, no, no," she told him shaking her head. "He wouldn't have done this. Besides, men aren't usually that destructive. That's something that a woman would do. And since I am not dating anyone, it can't be a jealous girlfriend or anything like that. Maybe whoever it was, had mistaken my car for someone else's."

Not convinced, Anderson asked again. "You're sure it couldn't have been that the guy from the reception? And how do you know he isn't capable of damaging your car out of spite? You did say you gave him the treatment after he insulted you." Anderson knew how rough Taylor could be with those who crossed her.

Sighing, Taylor knew she had better tell him the whole story before Dain found himself on the business end of an arrest warrant.

"Anderson the rude guy at the reception was Dani's brother, Dain. I didn't learn who he was until afterward the party when I ran into him again at *Beautiful Colors*."

Anderson's eyebrows instantly rose after hearing Dain's name, but he said nothing.

"Do you really think that he is capable of doing such a thing?" Taylor didn't think Dain was capable, but she wanted Anderson's opinion of him.

Still not commenting, he let her continue. He didn't know what to make of this revelation, but he wanted to learn more.

"Besides, I forgave him for his transgressions," Taylor admitted.

"When did all of this take place?" Anderson asked, not liking where this was headed, considering Dain was currently sleeping with his sister.

"The night of Dani's dinner party, he was the reason that I didn't attend," she confided.

"That doesn't make any sense Taylor, Dain was at the party," he informed her, clearly confused.

"Yes, I know."

Taylor explained to Anderson how she encountered Dain as she was arriving and he was leaving. She told him how he practically begged her to leave with him and how they ended up talking all night at a nearby coffee shop. She further explained that he asked for forgiveness and that she had granted it.

Anderson was upset. Not only was Dain Sinclair sleeping with his sister, but from the looks of things, he was trying to crawl into Taylor's bed as well. What was it about that guy that women seemed to let him slide with his womanizing behavior? Even though Taylor assured him that she had no interest in Dain other than friendship, Anderson was not so sure that Dain had the same ideas. He made a mental note to add Dain Sinclair to the list of people he needed to make a personal visit to. In the meantime, he needed to get Taylor home and arrange for her car to be towed for repairs.

Chapter 13

"We need to talk," Anderson informed Dain as he pushed passed him.

"Well come right on in," Dain offered sarcastically. He frowned when he opened the door to Anderson. He immediately assumed that Mia had run to her big brother about him breaking things off with her.

Closing the door, he sighed. Following Anderson into the living room, Dain stood waiting for the blow that was sure to come. He couldn't believe Mia had pulled her brother into this mess.

"What do you want Anderson?" He asked after he didn't attempt to sit or take a swing at him.

"I want to know, what you're doing with my sister and cousin?" He asked.

"I'm not exactly sure what you're asking me, Anderson." Dain folded his arms, annoyed with his line of questioning.

"I know that you and Mia are sleeping together. I picked up that much from the dinner party. What I want to know is what are you trying to do with Taylor? Are you trying to add her to your list of conquests? I try to stay out of grown people's business, but—"

"As you should," Dain countered, clearly irritated with Anderson.

Ignoring him, Anderson continued. "But I draw the line when my cousin's car is smashed to hell!" Anderson finished.

"Taylor? Is she ok?" Alarmed, Dain unfolded his arms, genuinely concerned.

"She's fine no thanks to you; because I am sure, one of the many women that you have drop-kicked over the years had something to do with the damage to Taylor's car.

"And while we are on the subject of women, I don't know what kind of arrangement you have with Mia, but if you plan to pursue Taylor, you better break it off with her before you do. Unlike my brother, I let adults live their own adult lives, unless it becomes dangerous, as it has tonight. So make no mistake, if either Mia or Taylor gets caught up in one of your deranged hussies' plans, I will be back," Anderson promised before he made his way to the door to leave.

"Anderson, I broke it off with Mia days ago. It was only that one time so…"

"Glad to hear it, but I don't need to know the gory details," Anderson interrupted.

Dain continued. "I just want you to know that it's different with Taylor. She's different than any woman I have known. I wouldn't do anything to hurt her or let anyone else hurt her."

"What about my sister?" Anderson asked.

Dain sighed. "Anderson, Mia is not who you think she is. She may come off all sweet and naive, but she's not. She's a great girl and all, but something is going on with her," Dain informed him.

"Just remember what I said, Dain." Anderson continued to the door, letting himself out; not really wanting to hear about Mia's transgressions.

However, on the way to his car, Anderson considered what Dain said about Mia. He knew that there was much he didn't know about his sister, he also suspected what Dain said was true. If that was the case, could Mia have been the one who damaged Taylor's car?

No, couldn't be, he thought. With all the women Dain has been through, it had to be a nut job from Dain's past. Besides, Taylor said that no one knew she left with Dain that night. They were the only ones outside.

Finally dismissing the idea that Mia was responsible for Taylor's car, Anderson slid into his car to make the second stop of the night.

****

After Anderson left, Dain grabbed his keys. He had to make sure that Taylor was okay. Backing out of his driveway, he had the uneasy feeling that Mia was the responsible party for Taylor's damaged car. Sure he had dated some women who became combative after he no longer wanted to see them, but that was ages ago, which made it more feasible that Mia was involved. Maybe not, he thought shaking his head, it could have nothing to do with him at all.

Chapter 14

Anderson knocked on the second door of the night.
He stared at Jayden whom he had called to meet him, after
leaving Dain's place. He just hoped that Jayden could keep
his cool and his fists to himself. It was time that they paid a
little visit to their father. Anderson knocked again after not
getting an immediate response to the first one.

Anderson had tried hiring the private investigator
that he had commissioned years ago to find his father a
second time, only to learn that the man had retired.
However, he had recommended his replacement, an ex-
army man, who after checking around, Anderson found to
be reliable and excellent at his job. Finding Rendell the first
time had been difficult for Anderson, after learning about
his other family. This time he had needed Rendell's
whereabouts to protect his mother.

The door finally opened to a very tired and
haggardly-looking Rendell. Anderson and Jayden
exchanged glances before they entered the suite, neither
saying a word as they did so. Rendell closed the door,
wondering why his sons were there, although he could
guess from their expressions that this was not a social call.

Anderson spoke first. "We are here for one thing and one thing only, to make sure that you stay away from Adaisha."

Rendell dropped into the chair that he had been sitting in before he let his sons inside. He'd had about all he could take and was weary of the whole situation.

"You boys could have saved yourself a trip. Your mother's husband made it quite clear what he would do to me if I approached his wife again."

Jayden and Anderson looked at each other again, finding a new respect for their stepfather.

"But if you two want to add your threats go right ahead. But know this, I won't be bothering any of you again. You all have made your point. I am not welcome in your lives. I fully accept that, and I can only blame myself. So if that is all, I have some packing to do. It's time that I go home."

Not having anything else to add, the brothers left Rendell to his packing.

"Well that was easy," Jayden remarked while he and his brother walked to their cars. "Do you think that he was telling the truth about leaving mom alone?"

"Strangely enough I believe him. I don't think he wants to tangle with Matthew. However, I believe somewhere in that selfish mind of his, Rendell thought that he could get his family back, with mom included. With Matthew showing up informing him that he was her husband and that he wasn't having any of his nonsense, squashed that delusion," Anderson predicted with Jayden nodding his agreement.

****

"I'm so glad that you are ok," Dain told Taylor. He had broken all kinds of traffic laws trying to get to her place. He had to see for himself that she was unharmed.

"As you can see Dain, I'm fine. I'm just a little shaken up that's all. Never in a million years would I have expected something like that to happen to me. I don't have any enemies."

Dain listened and for the second time that night, he couldn't help but wonder if Mia was involved. Although he believed he had gotten Taylor away from Dani's house in

time, he couldn't be sure that no one saw them. What if
Mia noticed that he had left, and had come outside looking
for him? He couldn't be certain she hadn't. Even though
she said she understood and accepted the rules of the game,
could she be capable of harming Taylor? He would like to
think not.

"As I told Anderson, I don't think that it was about
me. I believe someone may have gotten my car confused
with someone else's." Taylor was sure of it and Dain hoped
that she was right.

"Hey, how did you know about the incident
anyway?" Taylor suddenly asked.

Mentally Dain slapped his forehead. Now he would
have to tell her about the visit from her cousin.

"Well, to make a long story short, Anderson was a
little concerned that we were together the other night. He
wanted to make sure that I wasn't trying to take advantage
of you." Dain admitted. He hoped Anderson's concerns
wouldn't scare her off.

Rolling her eyes, Taylor replied, "Family or not
Anderson and Jayden are just too over-the-top with their
concerns." She threw up her hands. "I told him that

everything was okay between us. He had no right to confront you, I'm sorry," she added embarrassed.

"It's okay." He shrugged. "I paid a call to Devin when he and Dani started dating. That's just what we men do for the ones we love," he said with a chuckle. Taylor laughed with him.

"I know that we are supposed to have dinner later this week, but after what happened today, how about I take you to dinner tonight? You're a little tense and I know the perfect place that serves great food with a calming atmosphere."

Eyeing Dain with skepticism, Taylor asked, "You're not suggesting that we go to your place are you?"

"You know, I deserve that, but no. It's a genuine restaurant that I think you will enjoy. How about it?" He asked hopefully.

"Sure, why not? Just give me a few minutes to change." Taylor sauntered off, leaving a very relieved Dain sitting in her living room.

Glad that she accepted his offer, he expelled a breath he hadn't realized he was holding. He enjoyed spending time with Taylor. She was an amazing woman. He liked her easygoing personality. There were no games or manipulations from either of them, making it possible for him to relax and be himself. He didn't have to pretend to be interested in what she was saying just to get her into bed. With Taylor, it was just good company. Something he never wanted before.

"OK, I'm ready."

"After you, my lady," Dain replied with a smile.

#

"Wow," Taylor exclaimed after taking her first bite of food. Closing her eyes, she chewed slowly savoring the flavor. "This gumbo is delicious. It is by far the best I've eaten."

Dain had brought her to his favorite Cajun-Creole restaurant. Not able to decide on any one dish, he ordered several, to give Taylor a variety of some of his favorites. Along with the gumbo, they shared red beans and rice, jambalaya, and his favorite dish, seafood Newburg.

"I'm glad that you accepted my invitation to dinner tonight," Dain expressed between bites of his jambalaya. "I must admit I was worried after Anderson told me what happened."

"Nothing like that has ever happened to me before, which makes me believe that this whole thing has to be a fluke. It's not like I'm dating with some jealous woman out there seeking revenge over her man." Taylor added with a chuckle.

Outwardly Dain smiled, inwardly he wasn't so sure that a jealous woman wasn't involved, dating or not.

"Well if it isn't Captain Dain Sinclair."

A woman suddenly appeared at their table sing-songing Dain's name. "Is this your latest victim?" She asked thumbing towards Taylor. "I bet you never thought you would see me again, did you, Dain? Not waiting for an answer, the woman turned towards Taylor.

"Honey, if I were you, I would get as far away from this man as you can possibly get. If you're looking for bad news, you will find this man right in the thick of it."

Without waiting for either of them to reply, the woman gave Dain one last distasteful glare, before she sashayed on her way.

"I guess you've hurt a few feelings along the way, huh," Taylor commented, amused. She was by no means delusional about the type of man that Dain was. It was clear to her the night they met.

"Listen Taylor…." Dain started only to be interrupted by yet another woman.

"Dain! I thought that was you sitting over here. You said that you would call so we could hang out sometimes. Why haven't you called?" The irate woman asked. "You shouldn't have asked for my phone number if you had no intentions of using it. I don't give my number out to just anybody."

Taylor sat back in her chair arms folded, curious to know how Dain would talk his way out of this one. She watched him ask "Bella" to have a word with him in private. Somewhat satisfied, the woman preceded him to the lobby of the restaurant, but not before she gave Taylor the once over. Taylor observed them as they appeared to be having a heated conversation at first, but seconds later the woman left smiling.

"I do apologize for the interruptions this evening. As you can tell they were very unexpected," Dain explained when he returned to their table. "I've never brought a date here, so it's very unusual that I would run into anyone that I know."

"Dain you don't owe me any explanations. We aren't dating, and I'm not your wife or girlfriend. I must say though, your life must be very complicated, with all the women that you juggle. What did you tell Ms. Bella that she left without resistance?"

Embarrassed, Dain had no idea that their simple dinner would turn into something so complicated. For the first time, he began to see how his behavior with women was not a good thing. He wanted Taylor to see him as a man she could be proud to know, not the misogynist jerk that he was quickly becoming ashamed of. It never bothered him before if a woman confronted him about his bad behavior. He would always shrug it off and move on to the next woman. However, tonight Taylor was a witness to his crimes and he was deeply ashamed.

"I told her that I would call her later to explain," he admitted quietly.

Reaching across the table, Taylor touched his hand. "It's ok. Like I said, I know who you are. I got a firsthand introduction, remember?"

"Taylor, that's what I wanted to talk to you about. I don't want to be that person that you met that night. I look back on not just that night, but also my behavior in general, and for the first time, I don't like what I see. Tonight, with those women, has just added to it. I realize that I need to make some serious changes in my life." He meant it and just hoped she would stick around during the process.

Squeezing his hand, Taylor responded, "Dain, I hope for your sake that you are sincere in making a change because, in the long run, your deeds will only bring you trouble. For what it's worth, you can count me as a friend. Despite everything, heaven help me, I do like you," She added with a smile.

Feeling better since the interruptions, Dain smiled back.

Chapter 15

Anderson looked up from the brief he was writing to find Dain standing in his doorway. "What's up Anderson, I'm here to pick up Taylor for lunch," he informed him.

"Come in and close the door, Dain. Taylor went to the post office. She will be right back" he responded.

Despite his and Dani's disapproval, Dain and Taylor had become good friends. Taylor had reassured Anderson that she and Dain were only friends and that he had nothing to worry about, but still, he needed to be certain.

As he was told, Dain closed the door and sat down in a nearby chair, certain he knew what was coming next. He had already gotten the talk from his sister concerning his relationship with Taylor. Dani pleaded with him to leave Taylor alone friend or not, especially if he had plans to treat her like his usual women. He assured his sister, as he would Anderson, again, that was not the case. He genuinely cared for Taylor and he valued her too much to mistreat her in any way.

"I'm sure you're aware of what Taylor has told me about your relationship, but I want to hear from you. I also understand we've had this conversation before, but that was before you two became so close. What's going on Dain? And before you say it's none of my business, know this. I take family very seriously, so when I see one of them about to make a mistake I speak up. Taylor may say friends now, but women are women. Their feelings are often involved whether you like it or not."

"Anderson, I understand where you're coming from. As I told you before, you don't have to worry about Taylor. I have nothing but respect for her and will not do anything to hurt her. We are friends and friends only...though," he hesitated, "I will admit to you that I would like for that to change someday. Only if that is what she wants," he quickly added after Anderson was poised to object.

"Anderson I have come to care a lot about your cousin, so much so that I have left all other women alone. Although we aren't technically dating, I enjoy her company and her friendship, something that I hadn't realized I wanted in a woman."

Dain shared this with Anderson, not realizing he had revealed he was falling for Taylor, something Anderson didn't think Dain realized about himself. He recognized the look. He possessed the same expression when he fell for Paige. However, he had to be sure.

"And what about my sister Dain?"

"Anderson, Mia is not part of the equation. As I said before, it was a one-time thing. I know how that sounds, but at the time, I was the Dain of the past. I haven't been with her since. I realized that it was a mistake immediately and that's why I ended it. I sincerely hope you won't hold that against me," he replied.

Sighing, Anderson leaned back into his chair in thought. He wanted to believe Dain was a changed man. Although he understood he was falling for Taylor, he wondered what would happen once Dain realized this. Would he run as some men do? He didn't want to see Taylor hurt. As for his sister, Anderson had asked Mia about her relationship with him and she too assured him they didn't have a relationship. She had parroted Dain, stating that it was a one-time event and that she was fine with it. Still, he wasn't so sure she wasn't involved in the damage to Taylor's car.

"Dain, I am going to take you at your word, but hear me and hear me good. If you hurt Taylor, you will have to deal with me." Anderson repeated his previous threat, with Dain nodding his understanding. Anderson knew he sounded like his brother Jayden, but at least he was willing to give the man a fair shake before he talked with his fists.

Taylor lightly knocked on the door before letting herself into Anderson's office. "There you are," she said to Dain.

Eyeing both the men, Taylor wondered if the conversation had been about her. Knowing her cousin, she was sure it had been.

To Anderson, she asked, "Is everything okay in here?"

"Everything is fine. You two go on to lunch." He assured her with a wink.

Taking this as his acceptance of their friendship, Taylor smiled.

Chapter 16

Anderson had a right to be concerned about Mia. After discovering Dain and Taylor's causal relationship, she was enraged. She wanted Dain for herself. She had nothing against Taylor, however, Mia felt she was better suited for Dain than Taylor or any woman for that matter.

When Anderson asked her about her tryst with Dain, Mia felt insulted, because, for her, it wasn't a one-time hookup. In her mind, she and Dain had connected. Although she did not mention this so-called connection to Anderson, nevertheless, it was real for her. So when asked, she just went along with the causal hookup narrative that everyone expected her to have agreed to.

But she didn't agree, not in heart. At the time she would have agreed to anything to climb into bed with Dain. She had to figure out a way to make them all see they were meant to be together. She just couldn't understand why Dain didn't feel it. In her mind, he had to be ignoring their special bond, but she would change that.

Mia had been following Dain for a while. She felt it was necessary after tailing him to Taylor's house after she vandalized her car. She had followed them to some hole-in-the-wall restaurant. She was grateful the place was crowded which enabled her to keep an eye on them without being noticed by either.

She caught the scene between Dain and the two women who confronted him. She was sure the incidents would scare dainty Taylor off, but no such luck. Taylor had taken in the episodes amused. Mia didn't understand that. If it were her sitting there with Dain, with random women interrupting their meal, she would have scratched their eyes out. This led her to believe that maybe Dain and Taylor's relationship was nothing more than platonic, which pleased her to no end.

Today, however, was different. It was the first time Dain had gone to her brother's office for Taylor. And since he wasn't nursing a black eye and had Taylor in tow, did that mean Anderson approved of their relationship? Mia became more anxious because she knew if something wasn't done soon, they would become more than buddies. This would make it more difficult to persuade Dain that they belonged together. She had to form a new plan. Pulling her phone from her purse, Mia called for help.

#

Placing the phone back onto its cradle, Rendell was disturbed. His daughter was out of control and it was his fault. In the past, he had turned a blind eye to Mia's habits with men. He saw how she flirted with them and how she would come home in the early hours of the morning, whenever she visited him.

Rendell was loathed to accept that Mia was her mother's daughter, with all of Miranda's whorish ways. On top of that, his selfish pursuit of his family had inadvertently taught Mia that whatever she wanted she could have by any means necessary. After speaking with her today, he would have to face facts. Even though Mia took after her mother, he was the catalyst for her destructive behavior. He could have put a stop to it years ago. But he was so wrapped in his own self-pity, that he hadn't realized how far she had taken this behavior.

Mia wanted him to help her convince this Dain person that they should be together. He tried to get her to understand, that if the man didn't want her, she had to accept that. Mia wouldn't hear of it. She had scolded him for giving up on getting his family back and that she would not give in so hastily as he had done.

Rendell had no idea that his daughter had become as selfish and determined as he had been. He saw that now. Realization as to who he was had finally sunk in after he had to give up the fight for his family. Especially after Adaisha's husband, Matthew had shown up. He had no idea that Adaisha had remarried. She had been a key part of his plan to reunite his family. All his plans were crushed, once Matthew made it clear that he would protect Adaisha at all costs. Without her, his sons would forever be lost to him. He had to accept that reality.

Resigned, Rendell sat down in his favorite chair, deep in thought on how to help his daughter to understand, that she couldn't make someone want or love her. Either they did or they didn't. He had to try to get through to her before she destroyed herself or others.

****

Concluding that her father was no help, Mia was on her own. Just as well she thought. She would be free to do as she saw fit to acquire Dain. Giving up on her father, Mia decided she needed to bump up her tactics. She felt the key to winning back Dain was through Taylor. If she could frighten her into leaving him, her path would be free and clear.

Mia decided not to follow them after leaving Anderson's office but drove to Taylor's home instead. She let herself in by forcing open a window at the back of the house. Once inside, she wandered around Taylor's home, poking into drawers, and sorting through clothes and accessories in Taylor's dressing room, deciding Taylor had good taste.

Rummaging through the rest of the house, Mia saw touches of Paige's decorative work throughout. She decided she should have her sister-in-law decorate her apartment. With each room she visited, she was in awe of the décor and artwork and had to admit, Taylor had excellent taste.

Having wandered throughout the home, with no intent other than to gather information on her competition, Mia was about to leave when she spotted a colorful bouquet on a table near the front door. Curious, she picked up the card resting near the crystal vase of flowers, and read the card aloud.

"To my favorite girl,

Thank you for giving me a chance."

Dain

Mia was beside herself. Is Dain sending her flowers now? What was going on between them? Not liking what she was thinking, she flung the vase of flowers across the room.

"His favorite girl?" She screamed.

Infuriated, Mia shoved the remainder of the objects gracing the antique table to the floor. Moving about the room, she destroyed several more of Taylor's nice things, not in the least concerned over the mess she made or the trouble it could cause.

Mia halted her destruction long enough to pace the floor to calm herself. How could she make all of this go away? What could she do to break Dain's attachment to Taylor? She had to think. There had to be something she could do. There had to be.

Coming to her senses, Mia rolled her shoulders, quickly realizing that she needed to leave. Taking one last look at the mess that she made, she left the way that she came in, through the window.

After making her way to the front of the house, Mia glanced around to make sure that she hadn't been seen climbing from the window. Moving swiftly, she made her way down the block to her car. Glancing around once more, she let out a sigh of relief, certain that she wasn't seen or heard. With a small grin, Mia, pleased with her handy work, started her car and left Taylor's neighborhood.

Slumped in his seat as she drove past, the man following Mia had witnessed it all. Pulling away from the curb, he continued his task of tailing his assignment.

#

Tor Hudson had shaken his head in disbelief as he watched Mia pry open Taylor Patterson's kitchen window.

"This woman is off the chain," he muttered as he positioned his iPhone to capture her climbing inside. After leaving his car, he had to sprint through the adjacent alley to catch her in the act.

His employer had asked that he only document her activities and not interfere unless the situation became life-threatening. Tor thought that his employer was making a mistake because this woman had committed several criminal acts since he started following her.

Tor Hudson was a private investigator who freelanced whenever Graham Security Inc. was not paying him for his services. Justin Graham only used him for especially difficult jobs. Although high paying, they were usually dangerous.

Tor had plans to start his own small firm in a few months, something that he was looking forward to accomplishing. He was more than ready to ride a desk and delegate assignments instead of working on them himself. He'd had enough of the cloak-and-dagger jobs from serving as a member of military intelligence for the army.

Only in his mid-thirties, he had retired early, burnt out from difficult and stressful missions. Although he did not miss the grueling tasks of the military, he questioned if walking away from the sometimes difficult work at Graham Inc. would be in his best interest, especially after following this crazy woman.

After Mia entered the house, Tor positioned himself at a side window where he observed her strolling from room to room, pulling open drawers, and rifling through closets. With nothing eventful, he saw her finally making her way toward the back of the house. He was relieved. But that relief was short-lived.

Assuming she was heading back to her entry point, Tor was preparing to make his way back to his car, when he saw her abruptly stop in mid-stride. Not knowing what to expect, he instinctively raised his phone, capturing her tossing a vase of flowers across the room. In disbelief, he let the video continue as he watched her tear the room apart. Satisfied he had gotten enough for now, he hurried to his car to wait for Mia to return to hers.

While he waited for his target, he attached the video to an email. As an afterthought, Tor asked his client if he should get the police involved, before hitting the send button.

He started following Mia Stone after his client learned of the vandalism to Taylor's car. The man didn't know at the time who was responsible but was anxious to find the culprit. Tor was first commissioned to follow Taylor. However, after spotting Mia tailing her, along with a second person, Dain Sinclair, his client directed him to stick with Mia instead.

Tor had reported the details of Mia's escapades ever since. He had watched her enter Sinclair's home a few times, while he was away. To Tor, she seemed to be fixated on the man. Sometimes she would sit out in the airport baggage claim or the parking lot just to follow him. She would be particularly interested when Dain would be with Taylor. This seemed to set her off, sending her into one of what Tor called her "excursions," which included letting herself inside Dain's house. Sometimes she would undress and put on one of the man's shirts and lay on his bed, pleasuring herself. Whenever she would do this, Tor would go back to his car to wait. He was an investigator, not a voyeur. Besides, Mia's behavior greatly disturbed him.

His phone chimed. He had a new message. Tor sighed in frustration at the reply to his email. He was not to do anything but observe.

Tor's first request to involve the police was after Mia's first unlawful entry into Dain's home, after which he received the same answer. He could only hope the client knew what he was doing because he didn't want to be responsible if this woman decided to do more than destroy property.

Catching movement in his rearview mirror, he spotted Mia hurrying to her car. Slumping down in his seat, he waited until she drove past before he started his car to follow.

Chapter 17

"Oh my God! Dain! Someone's been inside my house!" Taylor was near hysterics. She had gotten home from work to find some of the contents of her home scattered all over her living room floor.

"Taylor, get out of there now and call the police!" Dain directed her. "I'm on my way!"

He couldn't believe that this was happening. First her car now her home? What was going on?

Racing to his car, Dain had a sick feeling that none of this was a coincidence. Taylor's troubles did not start until they started seeing each other. Mia came to mind again. Could she be capable of doing such a thing? If not Mia, did Taylor have someone in her past that was out to hurt her? All of these thoughts ran through Dain's mind as he sped over to Taylor's place.

Skidding to a stop, he bound from his car, sprinting to a shaken Taylor just as the police were arriving.

"Baby, are you ok?" He asked worried.

Dain grabbed her, hugging her with more concern than ever. Taylor was frightened. Feeling her shriveling, he held her from him, searching her body for any injuries. Satisfied that she was unharmed, at least physically, he embraced her again.

"Excuse me, folks, could someone tell us what happened?" One of the police officers asked once they reached the pair standing in Taylor's yard.

#

Dain had finished clearing the last of the glass and water from the broken vase. He had cleaned up most of the debris while Taylor was in the shower. He convinced her that she needed to relax, promising he would take care of the mess.

The police had gone over every room looking for clues as to who may have broken into her home. They took photos of the destruction and the tool marks on a kitchen window, the apparent entry of the intruder. With Dain by her side, Taylor had gone through the house noting that nothing had been taken. It appeared the only room disturbed was the common room.

Padding back into the room in a white terry cloth robe, Taylor hugged herself as she watched Dain place broken glass in the trash.

"Why the hell is this happening to me, Dain? First my car, now this?"

Placing the broom and dustpan against a wall, he pulled her into his arms. "I don't know baby, but I plan to find out. In the meantime, why don't you pack a bag and come home with me? First thing in the morning I will have a security system installed, so this doesn't happen again."

Nodding, Taylor left to do what he suggested.

Breathing a sigh of relief, that she hadn't fought him on his suggestion of coming to his place, Dain drew his hand down his worried face. Who was doing this to her? Was his assumption correct that this was Mia's handy work? Retrieving his phone from his back pocket, he called Anderson.

#

Anderson was also worried. After speaking with Dain, he tried calling Mia only to get her voicemail. He hated to admit it, but he had to agree with Dain. Mia may have had something to do with what was going on with Taylor after all.

He had tried getting together with her on numerous occasions for dinner or lunch, but she always gave him some excuse as to why she couldn't meet with him. He had stopped by her home a couple of times, but no response. He knew she was angry with him and Jayden because of Rendell and had just chalked it up to that. He assumed that she would come around eventually. However, after learning what had taken place at Taylor's home, he wasn't so sure that was the only reason she was avoiding him.

"Anderson, what's wrong?" Paige asked her husband as she sat down beside him.

Paige was still unaware of what had taken place with Taylor, Dain, and Mia. Before now, he hadn't believed it was important enough to mention.

"I'm worried about Mia," he admitted. "Some things have happened, which have me concerned that she may be in trouble," he told her.

"In trouble, what kind of trouble? Tell me," she pleaded.

Sighing heavily, Anderson gave Paige a blow-by-blow account of what had taken place with Dani's brother and Mia. He then explained the close relationship that had budded between Taylor and Dain. How Dain was falling for Taylor, although he didn't believe Dain was aware of that fact. He further explained why he suspected Mia of all the things that were happening to Taylor. Anderson also confided that Jayden was unaware of any of it and that he preferred to keep it that way, at least for now.

"Wow. I had no idea all of this was going on. Dani never mentioned a word to me about any of it. Why?" She asked her husband.

"Babe, don't blame Dani. She thought if things went badly between Dain and Mia or Dain and Taylor it would put a strain on your friendship. Besides, I told her that I would monitor the situation, and if there was anything to tell, I would be the one to tell you."

"Well, I know you mentioned that Jayden doesn't know, but does Andee know what's been going on?" Paige was overwhelmed with all the information she just learned.

"I think that she knows about Dain sleeping with Mia but not about what has been going on with Dain and

Taylor. Taylor, knowing how most of us feel about Dain's past, thought it best to keep quiet about their relationship, even if it is a platonic one. She didn't want to hear the warnings. She wanted to follow her own lead."

"Paige," Anderson added shaking his head, "although Taylor says she and Dain are just friends, I believe she is falling for him as well. I just hope for everyone's sake that Dain will step up and do the right thing and not abandon her when she finally does reveal her feelings."

"Why are you worried? You said Dain was falling for Taylor, so what is the problem?" Paige asked confused.

"Baby some men...men like Dain, when they realize they are falling in love, they tend to run in the opposite direction. They feel as if they are losing control and can't handle it. So instead of giving in to their hearts, they run, leaving the woman to suffer. I just don't know if Dain has it in him to stick around. I would like to think that he does, but I just don't know." Shaking his head again, Anderson pulled Paige into his arms.

"What are you going to do about Mia?"

"I don't know. I really don't know."

****

Mia could not believe that Taylor was staying with Dain. He had moved her right on in after she made a mess of her home. Had she known the bastard would take Taylor home, she would have never gone inside of Taylor's house let alone trashed it.

She had driven back to Taylor's, to catch the fireworks that were sure to come after Miss Prissy discovered the mess she had left behind. She didn't have to wait long before Taylor came barreling out of the house in hysterics.

"That ought to do it," she had said grinning while congratulating herself. Mia sat in her car smiling smugly while she watched Taylor pace back and forth in her yard, presumably waiting for the police and probably Anderson.

However, to her astonishment, Anderson was not the one to show up, Dain had. Mia's jaw dropped as she watched Dain race from his car to get to the distraught Taylor. She watched him gather her into his arms, comforting her. He held her so tenderly as if she were the most precious thing on earth to him. Mia was furious.

She couldn't understand what he saw in Taylor. Sure, she was pretty, but she was too ladylike for a man like Dain. He needed someone full of fire. Someone he could walk the razor's edge with; that was not Taylor. Mia could not imagine Taylor doing some of the things she and Dain had indulged in, posted up in New York.

"That's why he needs me," she whispered to herself. "Dain needs a woman who can handle him, who understands him. Taylor wouldn't begin to know what to do with him." She smirked knowingly.

Wanting to see what he would do next, Mia had waited not knowing what to expect. Her eyes widened when she spotted them coming out of the house with Dain carrying Taylor's overnight bag. She assumed that he was taking Taylor to Paige and Anderson's house. Just to be sure, she pulled away from the curb to follow them as they drove from the tree-lined block. Mia was so intent on following Dain, that she never noticed the dark sedan that fell in line behind her.

Keeping her distance, but still able to see Dain's car, she quickly realized that he wasn't taking Taylor to her brother's place. When they entered the freeway, she fretfully groaned as she wondered if he was taking her to his home. Once they exited the freeway leading to his house, she was sure of it.

Mia pounded the steering wheel in anger. "He's taking her home? No! This cannot be happening!" She drove past his house as he turned into his driveway and drove into the garage.

Chapter 18

"Are you comfortable?" Dain asked Taylor. They had made it back to his place where he ordered takeout; trying to take her mind off the break-in. They had just finished dinner and had moved into his media room for a movie with Taylor curled up next to him.

"I'm fine. I just can't get the sight of my home torn apart like that. I just don't get why this happening." The thought of this recent event made Taylor shiver. Someone was actually inside her home.

"Well, you're safe now and you can stay here as long as you like." He smiled when she looked up at him. "I made up the bed in the guest room for you," he added. He knew what she was thinking, but she didn't have to worry. He would not take advantage of the situation. He couldn't. He cared too much for her to do anything to jeopardize their relationship.

"I also made arrangements to have a security system installed first thing in the morning. I will drop you off at work and go back to your place to supervise the installation. I will also pick you up after work and take you wherever you want to go, be it here or home," He assured her, pulling her closer. He was relieved when he felt her finally relax. She should not have to endure this at all.

Dain was concerned. After his conversation with Anderson, he was more certain than ever that Mia was behind it all. He just hoped that Anderson could put a stop to it without Taylor finding out that he had slept with her. However, he didn't think that it would make a difference since it happened before they had become friends. Still, it wasn't his finest hour. It reinforced the appearance that he was prowling the reception looking for a bed partner, which he had been. But that was the old Dain. This Dain, Taylor's Dain, was much different.

Why couldn't he have listened to Dani and stayed away from Mia? He never thought his wild behavior with women would have caused this much trouble. He only had a couple of women to act out because of their parting, and they had always gone after him not anyone he was seeing. He had his tires slashed a couple of times, but nothing like this.

While Taylor was in the shower, he had tried calling Mia but had gotten her voicemail. He had to talk to her and find out what was going on with her. He needed to know if she was the one terrorizing Taylor. After speaking with her brother, he promised Anderson he would let him handle his sister. Dain hoped that he would be able to get the situation under control before she went off the deep end with somebody getting hurt physically.

Looking down at the woman in his arms, he realized that he would die protecting her. Dain didn't quite understand what was happening to him, but he found that he liked it.

#

Dain opened Taylor's door to his irate sister. Frowning, he motioned for her to come inside. He knew eventually Dani would find out what happened and would track him down.

"I knew your relationship with Taylor couldn't be good. Which one of your bimbos broke into Taylor's house?" Dani asked him with hands planted firmly on her hips. "Why couldn't you just stay away from Taylor? These things wouldn't be happening to her if it weren't for you, Dain," she scolded.

"Look Dani, if you're only here to give me grief you can just leave. You haven't said anything to me that I haven't said to myself, so if that's all," he said, gesturing towards the door she just entered. Before she could respond, the doorbell chimed.

"That would be the security company. Excuse me." Leaving Dani standing in the middle of the room, Dain moved to let the installers in.

Stepping aside to allow the men's entrance, Dani's eyes widened after she read the name of the company stenciled on the back of the workers' coveralls. She was livid. Pulling her brother into the kitchen while the men prepared to work, she let him have it.

"Out of all the damn companies that you could have chosen to install a security system, you had to choose Graham Inc?" Are you kidding me?" Dani whispered furiously at her brother.

"Dani, what the hell are you talking about?" Dain asked his sister, clearly confused and annoyed.

"Graham Inc, Justin Graham, does that ring a bell?" She asked him.

"Oh, shit!" Dain exclaimed, squeezing the back of his neck at his mistake. He had completely forgotten about the trouble Paige had with Justin Graham, owner of Graham Security.

Paige had dated Justin before she met Anderson. They had been hot and heavy until Paige discovered Justin had married another woman in the most awful way possible. She saw his wedding photo attached to a society article in the local newspaper. After Paige had gotten over him and had fallen for Anderson, Justin had shown up on their vacation drunk, trying to get back with Paige, while he was still married. Anderson had taken care of that little situation by beating the crab out of Justin and having him arrested.

Dain had completely forgotten the conflict. He was so worried about Taylor's safety that the name of the company, hadn't concerned with him.

"Well, they're here now, plus the company came highly recommended. Besides, Justin doesn't know me, Taylor, or our connection to Paige," Dain added. As far as he was concerned Justin Graham wasn't even remotely his problem.

Shaking her head, Dani couldn't believe the mess her brother had gotten himself into. He was right about Justin, but for now, her concern was with Taylor.

"What happened Dain? What did you do to cause all of this?" She gestured toward the working men.

"All I can tell you is, it's being taken care of, okay." He couldn't tell her that all of this probably stemmed from him sleeping with Mia. He didn't want to hear I told you so once again. He was already kicking himself over that decision.

"How did you find out about this anyway?" He asked her.

"Paige called me this morning to ask if I knew about the latest incident." Dain groaned. "Yes, little brother, Paige knows the whole story. You didn't think Anderson could keep it from her forever, did you?"

Listening to his sister as she went on and on about his escapades with "his women," led Dain to believe that Paige hadn't told her about his and Anderson's suspicions that Mia was behind it all. Knowing Anderson, Dain was sure that he had told Paige the complete story. He breathed a small sigh of relief. At least he had a small reprieve before Dani found out. He hoped by then, the Mia issue would have been solved.

Chapter 19

"I want to thank you for being such a good friend to me with all that has been happening," Taylor said as she and Dain rode the elevator down to the parking garage. "But now I think it's time that I go home. I can't stay with you forever," she told him with a chuckle.

Taylor had enjoyed her stay with Dain. She was glad she had given him a chance to redeem himself. The more time they spent together, the more, she liked him. If she were honest with herself, she would say that she loved him. Taylor smiled. She had to give him kudos for being the perfect gentleman. Not once did he cross the line, although there were times that she wished that he had. It was just as well. When the time was right for them to move to the next level, they both would know.

"Not a problem my lady, that's what friends are for."

They were leaving Anderson's office at the end of Taylor's workday. Even though Dain had secured Taylor's house, he had offered her an extended stay until she felt safe in returning home. To his surprise, she had accepted.

During her stay, he had taken a few days leave to accommodate her. He drove her to and from work and planned their evenings, which included dinner, movies or just playing video games at home. They had spent their time together growing closer. So close, he found himself on occasion taking cold showers in the middle of the night. Dain hated to see her leave.

Though he was comfortable in their friendship, Dain frowned. He often wondered if she would still consider him a friend if she knew he was more than likely the cause of her troubles. He considered telling her everything several times, but could never get the words out. He knew she deserved to know his suspicions and why, but he couldn't take the chance of jeopardizing it all, with the admission of his transgressions with Mia.

Reaching the garage level, they exited the elevator hand in hand, joking about the day's events. When they reached Dain's BMW, all of the humor was lost when they saw the word "Asshole" etched into the passenger side panel of his car in big bold letters.

"Son of a bitch!" Dain cursed at seeing his ruined car. Looking around the garage, hoping to catch a glimpse

of the person responsible for the deed, Dain let off a string
of profanity.

Horrified, Taylor tried pulling Dain back to the
elevator, but he wouldn't bulge. He was too upset to
consider the danger that they may be in.

"Dain please, let's go back upstairs and call the
police. They could still be down here," she pleaded.

"I hope they are," he yelled, looking around for who
was responsible. "I am tired of this shit! If you're here,
come out and face me you coward! Let's get this over with
once and for all!." Turning around in circles, Dain waited
to see if anyone would step forward.

"Dain please, this could be dangerous." Taylor was
frightened. Whoever was tormenting her had now turned on
Dain.

"Hey, what's the matter?" Anderson asked after
rounding the corner and finding them standing there.

"Oh, Anderson, thank God." Taylor was relieved to
see him, hoping he could talk some sense into Dain.
"Please tell him that we should get out of here. The vandals
could still be here," she explained pointing to Dain's car.

Anderson whistled at the damage. "Oh man, so she's started in on you now?" Anderson asked after examining Dain's car; forgetting that Taylor knew nothing of Mia's possible involvement.

"She? She who? Will one of you tell me what the hell is going on?" Taylor demanded, letting her gaze swing equally between the two men.

"Ugh!" Was all Dain could utter in frustration. He knew that he would have to come clean about everything now. He looked over at Anderson who only shrugged his apology for letting it slip.

"Look, why don't you take Taylor back upstairs and I will call the police. You two need to talk," Anderson suggested.

Realizing that he had no other choice, Dain grasped Taylors elbow guiding her back to the elevator. They didn't speak while they rode up to Anderson's office. He wondered what she was thinking. Would she still want him in her life, after he explained his and Anderson's theory, as to who they suspected was behind all the vandalism and why? Or would she become so upset with him that she would never want to see him again?

Dain had dreaded this day. He wanted to kick himself for not having the guts to tell her sooner. He was so sure that Anderson would be able to reign in his little sister, making it possible for him to keep his secret. He just hoped after he explained everything, Taylor wouldn't be too angry with him. He valued their relationship and hoped that someday she would see him as more than a friend. He hoped that she could see him as her man.

Exiting the elevator, Taylor led the way back to Anderson's office, unlocking the door to let them inside. Closing the door behind them, Dain followed her past her desk into Anderson's office. Taylor made her way to a nearby brown leather sofa, dropping onto it she waited for Dain to explain.

"Ok Dain, you want to tell me what's going on now?" She looked up at him expectantly.

Closing his eyes briefly, he sighed and walked over to the wall of windows that held a serene view of the river below. Sighing again, he turned to face Taylor.

"Taylor listen," he started, "This is only speculation on mine and Anderson's part, but we think that Mia may be the one behind the vandalism." He watched her face for a reaction. She was puzzled.

"Mia, Mia Stone? Anderson and Jayden's sister Mia?" She asked perplexed. Dain nodded. "Why would Mia do all of these things? What motive would she have?" She asked him; not understanding the point of what he was trying to say.

Dain searched his mind for what he should tell her. Should he tell her the complete truth or a creative version? He quickly chose the latter. He didn't stop to think how this could come back to bite him in the ass later.

"Taylor, Mia has been pursuing me for a while. She has tried to entice me to be with her, but I have declined. Anderson and I believe she has been doing these things because I won't give in to what she wants. We believe she perceives you as a threat and that's why your car and home were vandalized. She wanted to scare you away in hopes that I would turn to her."

Dain paused before he continued. "I can only assume today's stunt was just another tactic to separate us. I'm sorry, I should have told you sooner, but we thought we could handle the situation without getting anyone else involved."

There, he told her. It was the truth. He just left out the part about him sleeping with Mia in New York. Dain hoped the omission would never become important enough for him to have to explain. Besides, his interaction with Mia happened during the time Taylor couldn't stand him.

Taylor shook her head. "I knew something was wrong with that girl," she remarked. "I've noticed small things about her since I met her. Mia is the type of woman who thinks because she's beautiful, she should have whatever or whomever she wants."

Shaking her head again, Taylor rose to hug Dain. "I know that you and Anderson mean well and want to protect me, but you could have told me. I know how to handle women like Miss Thing." Taylor was relieved now that she knew who and what the problem was.

"So, you're not mad?" Dain asked surprised by her reaction.

"Mad no, annoyed yes. I know you may think that I am a delicate flower, Dain Sinclair, but I can handle myself pretty well or did you forget?" She asked him.

At Dain's confusion, Taylor took a step back and looked up at him. Rolling her eyes, she reminded him. "The first time we met, Dain?"

Laughing, he remembered. Dain had forgotten how she had cut him down at the wedding reception, so much so, she had him questioning his self-esteem.

"How could I have forgotten your sharp tongue?" Pulling her back into his arms, he held her tight.

Dain was relieved. He had dodged a bullet. Still, he had this gnawing feeling that he should have told her everything. Pushing the thought from his mind, he continued to hold her, relieved that he still had her in his life.

Not knowing what to expect when he walked into his office, Anderson stuck his head through the doorway.

"Is everything ok in here?" He cautiously asked the couple.

"Yes, everything is fine," Taylor answered releasing Dain. "What do you plan to do about your sister, Anderson? The girl is out of control. Who stalks someone because they won't sleep with them?" Taylor shook her head exasperated.

"Don't worry Taylor. I will take care of it," he answered.

Anderson gave Dain the eye, after realizing that he hadn't told her everything. Sighing he shook his head. Anderson knew that it would come back to haunt him in the worst way.

When will he learn?

Chapter 20

Tor knew he wasn't supposed to interfere, but after watching Mia key "asshole" in large block letters into Dain Sinclair's car, he'd had enough. This woman was out of order and someone needed to put a stop to her reign of terror. He was just about to make his presence known when his phone vibrated in his pocket. Checking the caller display, Tor backed out of the garage and retraced his steps back to his car.

"Hello," he answered tightly. "Look man, this crazy female is out of control. She just keyed Sinclair's car." Listening, Tor swiped his hand down his face frustrated.

"I understand that you want me to just observe and document, but—" He listened again after he was interrupted. "Ok, ok, but know this, if she starts in on people, I'm dialing 911." Tor ended the call with annoyance.

Tor Hudson was to observe and gather information only. He shook his head in disbelief. Maybe the guy was collecting enough information to take to the police himself, he thought. Why else did he want all the photos, videos, and reports?

Feeling a little better about the situation, Tor impatiently tapped on the armrest, waiting for Mia to return to her car. Besides, his client promised that his part in this madness was nearly complete. He sure hoped so. If he weren't being paid a great deal of money to do this job, he would have terminated it a long time ago.

****

After keying Dains car, Mia angrily drove back to her apartment. Not knowing what to do next, she sat in her car for what seemed like hours, trying to plan her next attack. Still unsure as to what to do, she finally exited her car. She nearly ran up the stairs to her apartment, disgusted with the day's outcome. She was no closer to getting Dain back and it angered her. As she drew closer to her door, someone stepped out of the shadows to greet her.

"I wondered if you were coming home tonight." It was her brother Anderson.

"Hi Anderson," she greeted sweetly. Mia's heart was pounding wildly. She had a feeling she knew why he was there, so she had to play it cool so as not to give anything away.

"What brings you by?" She asked as she unlocked her door to let them inside.

Following Mia inside, Anderson closed the door behind him, before following her further into her apartment. Mia threw her keys into a basket on a nearby table, dropping her purse in a chair as she slipped out of her heels. Trying to appear calm, she turned to Anderson and offered him something to drink.

Declining, Anderson sat down and laid out why he was there. "Mia, there have been some mishaps with Dain and Taylor. I came by to ask if you know anything about that."

He observed her as she took in a deep breath, exhaling gently, trying to calm herself. He had hoped he was wrong about her, but after witnessing her slightly shaking hands and her overall demeanor, he was certain she was involved.

"Anderson, mishaps? What do you mean...and why would I be involved? She asked him, not quite meeting his eyes.

"First there was the vandalism to Taylor's car, then her house, and today the vandalism to Dain's car. You wouldn't know anything about that, would you?" He asked her again.

This time she appeared fully calm and in control. She looked him straight in the eye and denied it all. "No, I don't know anything about that. Why would I? I told you ages ago Dain means nothing to me. We had fun, it's over and that's the end of it. Besides, I didn't know that Dain and Taylor were seeing each other. If that's the case, good for them and I wish them all the luck in the world." She finished her denial while once again smiling sweetly.

Not buying it, Anderson thought maybe he should set the record straight about Dain and Taylor's relationship, in hopes that Mia would back off.

"They aren't exactly seeing each other, not in the conventional way. They are just good friends who happen to share the same interests and enjoy hanging out together that's all."

"Oh Anderson, you didn't have to explain that to me," she said waving him off as if what he said was absurd. "As I told you before, whatever Dain does is his business.

I'm not interested in what he has going on with Taylor or anyone else for that matter. The man is old news," she assured him.

"That's good to know," he answered, still not buying her act.

Anderson had only known Mia for a short time. He had first become aware he had a sister, after bumping into her and Rendell in a restaurant, while out on a date with Paige. However, he didn't have to know her for any length of time to know that she was lying. His sharp instincts recognized the signs of untruth immediately.

"I plan to make sure that Taylor is protected from whomever it may be that is harassing her. I've hired some people to watch her for a while, just to make sure that nothing else happens to her. I know that Dain had an alarm system installed in her home, but I want to be certain she is safe wherever she may be."

Looking at his watch, Anderson noted the time. "Well, I've taken up enough of your time. I better get on home, before Paige sends out the cavalry," he teased with a chuckle, hoping to lighten the moment.

"How about lunch sometime this week?" He asked hugging his sister.

"That would be great. I will call you and let you know when I'm free," Mia told him as she opened the door to let him out. "Oh and Anderson, I am sorry to hear about your cousin's troubles. I hope that Dain is being equally careful as well. There is so much going on in this city these days," she added, fishing.

"Dain can handle himself. I just want to make sure that Taylor is taken care of. Good night little Sis." With that, he was gone.

Mia closed her door and stomped back into the living room where she dropped down onto her red leather sofa, with her irritation returning.

"I'll just have to be more careful now. No more bothering little Miss Taylor. Damn!" She shouted, throwing one of her accent pillows across the room. With her plans hampered by Anderson's security measures, Mia decided that she would lay off Dain and Taylor for a while. Anderson is no fool, she thought. He suspected that she was responsible; he just couldn't prove it. Mia got up to prepare for bed, accepting that her hands were tied for now.

Chapter 21

Anderson was at a loss, after confirming that Mia was indeed the culprit behind Dain and Taylor's woes. Even though he knew it was her, he couldn't prove it, and there lay the problem. He hated to admit it, but he needed help. Mia was not going to stop and he knew it. There was only one person that he could turn to, the person who knew her best.

Resigned to a plan of action it was time to execute it. After getting off the plane, he rented a car and drove to the address he obtained from the investigator he hired. Out of all the people whom he knew, he never believed he would have to turn to Rendell for help, but he didn't have a choice.

After he visited with Mia, he had hoped her obsession with Dain would have ceased. She had stopped the vandalism, but she still made it a point to drive by Dain and Taylor's homes from time to time. He had hired a couple of guys he knew from college who owned a personal bodyguard service to shadow Taylor. They had reported seeing Mia a few times, but she never left her car. Either Mia didn't believe him about the security detail or she couldn't help herself. Either way, he wanted to get ahead of any future trouble.

Finding the address that he was looking for, Anderson parked and killed the engine. He sat outside his father's house wondering if he was doing the right thing. If he asked Rendell for help, would this give the old man hope that he had a place in his life? He would have to make it plain that he was there only as a last resort, to help Mia, before she wound up in jail or worse. Having stalled long enough, Anderson exited the car to face his father.

#

Rendell stirred when the doorbell chimed. He had dozed off watching some inane television show. It was early evening, the sun barely sinking into the horizon. He wasn't sure what the sound was that had awakened him, but he was grateful that it had. He rose from his chair to prepare himself a small meal. He was headed to the kitchen when the bell chimed again. Recognizing it as the sound that had awakened him, he changed direction, heading for the front door. Opening it, he was stunned to find Anderson on the other side.

Anderson and his father stood staring at each other. Rendell, because Anderson was the last person he expected to see and Anderson because he recognized himself in Rendell's image. He pondered what would have happened if his father had stuck around instead of leaving them all those years ago. What kind of influence would he have had on his life? Would he have become the man he is today? Pushing those thoughts aside, he cleared his throat.

"May I come in?" He asked his estranged father.

"Sure, sure son, come in." Rendell quickly moved aside to allow his son to enter his home, before Anderson changed his mind and walked away. He was overjoyed to see him.

Anderson stepped over the threshold into his father's home. A step, a few months ago he couldn't have imagined himself taking. He followed Rendell into his sitting room as the older man rambled on about refreshments, which he politely declined. He was inside his father's house. He couldn't believe it. Taking the pro-offered chair, Anderson sat down to explain his purpose for being there.

"I'm sure you are surprised to see me," he started, "As I am pretty much surprised to find myself here." Rendell was silent, waiting for him to continue. "I'm here because of Mia. She has done some things that I am concerned about and I don't know how to handle the situation."

"When you say some things, exactly what has she done?" Rendell asked him, suddenly becoming fearful for his daughter.

"She's been harassing, mom's niece Taylor and her friend Dain." Closing his eyes, Anderson rethought his statement. "That's not completely accurate. It's been more like terrorizing them. Mia has followed them around town; she's smashed Taylor's car windows, and broken into her home trashing it. The latest incident was the defacing of Dain's car."

Rendell sat back in his chair stunned at hearing what his daughter had been up to. He was afraid something like this would happen. He should have contacted Anderson the moment Mia called him about needing help with Dain. He swept his hand over his close-cropped gray hair before he spoke.

"I was afraid of this. She called me a couple of months ago about Dain...is it?" Anderson nodded. "I told her to let it go. I tried to explain to her if the man didn't want her, there wasn't anything she could do to change that fact. She became angry with me and hung up. I didn't hear from her for a couple of weeks, but when she did call, she said that everything was okay and that I didn't have to worry about her. I took her at her word. I should have called you, but.."

"But I wouldn't have accepted a call from you." Anderson finished the sentence for him.

Anderson sighed. He realized had he had a relationship with his father, he wouldn't have hesitated to call him about Mia. He thought about the last time that he had seen Rendell. He hadn't wanted anything to do with him, but now here he was asking for his help.

"I don't blame you for not calling. That one's on me. But I'm here now and I'm hoping that we can put our heads together and come up with a solution to help her." He told his father.

Rendell nodded, pleased that Anderson had sought out his help. "I was just about to prepare my evening meal.

I think better on a full stomach. Will you join me?" Rendell offered.

"Sure, why not?" Anderson replied, bringing a smile to the older man's face.

Chapter 22

"Hi Andee, is my sister in?" Dain asked.

"Is she expecting you?" Andee teased him. She knew Dani always made time for her brother, especially since he had been seeing Taylor. She wanted to stay informed of any mayhem Mia Stone may have caused.

"Go right in, she's not with a client.

"Thanks." Dain winked, before heading for his sister's office.

"Knock, knock, are you too busy to talk to me a minute?" Dain asked his sister.

"No come on in and close the door." Dain closed the door as he was told.

"So what brings you by? Hopefully, you have some good news for a change. Lord knows there has been enough trouble."

Grinning, Dain took a seat. "Well, I just wanted to touch base with you. It seems lately, we have only communicated when something bad has happened. I wanted to break that cycle and see you on a good note for a change."

Dani smiled in relief. Dain was right. Whenever they saw each other, it was after Mia had gone on one of her rampages.

"So no Mia episodes, I take it?" Dani asked. Paige had finally informed her friend, about Anderson's suspicions that Mia was the culprit behind all the vandalism.

"No not a one. I think she has moved on to some other poor sucker. At least I hope she has. But enough talk about Evilena. I came here to talk to you about Taylor. Dani, I think that I love her...no I know that I love her." Dain smiled, liking the sound of this.

Examining her brother carefully, she believed he was finally hooked. She smiled at the possibility of a loving monogamous Dain.

"Aww...My little brother is in love, how sweet," she teased. "Seriously Dain, I've never seen you like this. Love looks good on you." She nodded her approval. "Now to the important question, how does Taylor feel about you?"

"Well, that's why I'm here. This is all new to me, so how can I tell if she feels the same way? In my so-called relationships, I never stuck around long enough to recognize the signs of a woman in love. Lust I know, but not love. Look at me. It took a while for me to recognize it in myself." Dain was truly perplexed at his newfound fortune.

"I hate to tell you this, but only the woman herself can let you know for sure. But there are some signs to tell you if she is heading that way," she explained.

"Some signs like what?" He asked anxiously.

Dain really wanted to know if Taylor could love him. He knew how she felt about him in the beginning, but they had come a long way from that ugly scene. He found himself wanting her in ways he never knew existed.

Dani pondered his question. "Well, you spend a lot of time together right?" Dain nodded. "Ok, if a woman is into you, I mean really into you, she will light up whenever she sees you or hears your voice. She will become 'touchy-feely' as you guys like to call it, whenever she's with you. She will rest her hand on your arm, cup your face when she is trying to make a particularly sexy point, or rest her head on your shoulder when you are having quiet time together. She will also rest her hand on your knee and not grope you the way I've seen some of your Pick-me's do," she added rolling her eyes.

"But most of all, she will let you hold her for no special reason at all, other than she feels comfortable and safe in your arms." Dani thought she summed it up pretty well for her love-struck brother.

A huge grin spread over Dain's face. Taylor had done all of those things and more. If she wasn't in love with him, he felt she was damn sure close. Suddenly having an idea, Dain leaped to his feet. Leaning over his sister's desk, he kissed her forehead and ran out of her office without a word.

"Hey, where are you going?" Dani shouted after him.

After almost being knocked down by a rushing Dain, Andee came into Dani's office to get the scoop.

"What did you say to him that had him running out of here like a bat out of hell?" She asked.

"I really don't know. I was telling him how to tell if a woman is falling in love and without a word, he just ran out of here." Dani explained.

"Love and Dain in the same sentence? Now that's impressive. How did that conversation come about?"

"Andee, I am proud to announce, drum roll please, that my brother Dain Sinclair is finally in love."

"Wow, wonders never cease," Andee, commented in awe.

****

Dain was ecstatic. He had mentally slapped his forehead after Dani completed her summation. Taylor could very well be in love with him. He sat there listening to his sister's account, growing happier with each word. Why hadn't he recognized it before? She had behaved very differently than any woman he had known before her. That in itself was a telltale sign.

He got into his car and headed to Anderson's office. He needed to see Taylor. He wanted to experience that excitement that he had taken for granted whenever he was with her. He also wanted to invite her to go away with him.

He didn't know why he hadn't thought of it before. Then again, he knew why the idea hadn't readily come to him. All of the women in his past had been disposable. It was not an option for him to invite any woman for a romantic trip.

Parking his newly painted car on the street, a must after Mia had defaced it in the parking garage, Dain hurried into the building and the elevator. Pressing the button repeatedly, he was impatient to reach the fifth floor. Bounding from the elevator, he opened the door to the office to find Taylor deep in conversation on the phone. From the frown on her face, it was not a pleasant exchange.

Smiling when she noticed his arrival, Taylor pointed at the phone rolling her eyes. She gestured to him, indicating that she would be with him shortly. Finally hanging up from her call, Taylor threw up her hands exasperated. She thought she had put all the criticism about Dain behind her ages ago.

"What's the matter?" Dain asked her concerned.

"My brother Kylon. After not hearing from him in months, he called to question me about my relationship with you of all things," she informed him.

"I don't understand, we have never met so why all the grief?" Dain asked her suddenly annoyed.

"It seems a little birdie, namely Anderson has been filling him in on the events that have been happening around here, with you, me, and Mia. He had been questioning if it was safe for me to continue to see you since Mia is a loose cannon."

"Well, did you explain to him that Mia is no longer a problem?" Dain asked her. "We haven't heard a peep out of her for weeks now. She has moved on."

"Yes, I have explained all of that. But Dain, he's my brother and he just wants to make sure that I am safe and out of harm's way."

"Call him back. I would like to speak to him. I want him to understand that I care about you and would never let Mia or anyone else harm you." Dain wanted to make sure Taylor's brother understood the facts.

Taylor smiled at Dain's declaration for her. He cared for her. I bet he never said those words about any woman before, she thought. She didn't think that he was aware of what he had just said.

Unbeknownst to her, Dain was very much aware of what he said. He loved her and very soon, he would make her aware of that welcomed fact.

"I'm sorry to disappoint you, but I am unable to call him back. He is still out of the country and as you know, his whereabouts are never revealed under any circumstances. But not to worry, he promised to be home soon, so you will get to have your say in person," Taylor happily informed him.

Glancing around the office, Dain realized Anderson's office door was open. "Hey, where is Anderson?" He asked.

This was the first time that he had been in his office and he wasn't there. Normally he would have come out to say hello if he wasn't with a client.

"Anderson had some business to take care of out of town. He should be back tomorrow." Taylor informed him.

"Does that mean that you can leave early today?" He asked hopefully. He wanted to take her to an early dinner and maybe make plans for the idea that he had.

"Hey, why are you here?" I thought that you were flying out today," she asked him, realizing that he was supposed to be at work.

"I had a great idea. Why don't we take some time off and go somewhere fun? Let's go lounge on some beach, drink tropical drinks, and just relax. With all that has been happening over the past months, we deserve to have some unrestrained fun." Dain was excited about spending time alone and away from anyone who knew them.

"That sounds like heaven. I have just one question?"

"Sure, anything," Dain agreed, growing more excited by her response.

"Well maybe not just one question, maybe a couple of questions," she added.

"Yes, anything, what are your questions?" Dain was nearly fidgeting from foot to foot waiting for her questions.

"Can we put the trip off for a few weeks? And, can I have my own room?" Taylor wanted to get away with Dain, but she wasn't quite ready to take that next step in their relationship. Who knows, she may have changed her mind while they were away, but for now, she wasn't ready.

"Dain I love spending time with you and would love to lie on a beach with you, but I'm not quite ready to share a hotel room with you. Do you understand?" She asked, hoping that she hadn't hurt his feelings.

Dain was a little disappointed but was willing to agree to her terms. At least she agreed she would go. With a perfect romantic setting, she may change her mind. He knew that his past bad behavior was the reason for her hesitation, but he was willing to wait. He loved her just that much.

"For you my lady anything." Smiling, Dain assured her that he understood. "Now tell me where you would like to go."

Chapter 23

"How did your visit go with your father?" Paige asked her husband after joining her in the car. She had come to bring him home from the airport.

Anderson kissed her hello before responding. "It was interesting. I learned that I could sit in the same room with the man and not feel anger. We discussed Mia over a meal that he prepared, which was quite good, I might add."

Paige spotted a small smile from Anderson when he talked about Rendell's cooking.

"So I take it your love for cooking isn't such a random thing after all," she suggested. She was pleased that some of the tension surrounding him and his father had dissipated.

"No, I guess not. He's quite fond of cooking as well, something I never knew about him. There are many things that we discovered we hadn't known about each other."

"You know Paige, even though he had come off quite cocky when he was trying to get us to forgive him, I believe that he is genuinely sorry for the choices he made back then." Anderson shook his head in wonderment while he gazed out at the passing scenery.

"People do make mistakes. We are all human and before this life is over we are going to make many more," Paige pointed out. "I know the mistakes Rendell made may seem monumental, but that is where forgiveness comes in."

Taking his hand, Paige glanced over at her husband before she asked him an important question. "Have you made peace with your father, Anderson?"

He lifted her hand and kissed it. "It's a work in progress."

"Well, at least that's a start." Page smiled; overjoyed that now her husband could begin to heal.

#

Rendell stared out the window at a young father teaching his son to ride a bicycle without training wheels. He had taught Anderson the same feat before he left him and his mother. He remembered how happy his son had been after he had finally gotten the hang of balancing the bike without his help. He had cheered him on while

Adaisha had clapped from her seat on the front steps of their house.

Smiling, Rendell shook his head. He couldn't believe that Anderson, his son. had actually been inside his home, breaking bread with him. He had to admit he didn't know what to expect after opening his door and finding him standing there. At first thought, he had come to give him more grief about visiting his mother, but he hadn't visited Adaisha since that night he had shown up at her home. He was somewhat relieved to learn that was not the case.

Remembering why Anderson had come, Rendell frowned. His daughter was out of control. He had explained to Anderson why he felt the whole situation was entirely his fault. If he hadn't been so selfish in his own life, Mia wouldn't have felt free to do the things that she had done. Rendell had dug deep and apologized for all the heartache and hardship that he had brought upon both his families. He now understood the pain he caused.

Anderson had listened intently, struggling at first, but towards the end of his confession, he had nodded, too emotional to speak. That moment had been emotional for the both of them. Rendell had found himself wiping tears from his own eyes. His son hadn't outright forgiven him, but he had become less rigid by the end of his stay.

"At least that was something," Rendell whispered to himself. "At least that was something."

Wiping a tear from his eye, he turned from the window to the task at hand. He sighed as he made his way into his bedroom to pack a small overnight bag. He had promised Anderson that he would meet him at Mia's apartment the next afternoon. He had a plane to catch. It was time that his wayward daughter got a lesson in reality.

#

Mia couldn't believe that Anderson had gone to their father about her so-called behavior. She was livid after receiving a surprise visit from Rendell accompanied by Anderson of all people. She had just gotten in from work and was trying to decide if she should make a sweep by Dain and Taylor's places to see what they were doing. She may not be able to enter Taylor's home, but that didn't stop her from driving through her neighborhood.

She knew about the men who pretended to be a part of Taylor's block. She had spotted them on her second tour, after keying Dain's car. Mia felt as long as she didn't leave her car, they couldn't do anything to her. It wasn't against the law to drive down the street.

A couple of times that she had driven by Taylor's home, she found Dain's car parked in her driveway. She would have given anything to know what was going on inside. Had they slept together? She wondered. She hadn't given up on Dain. She figured eventually he would revert to his old ways, and she would be there waiting when Taylor threw him out. It was only a matter of time. People like her and Dain, needed a certain element of excitement in their lives, an excitement that Taylor didn't possess.

What was she going to do now? Anderson and her father had threatened to get the authorities involved if she didn't stop her midnight cruises. However, she felt their threats were empty because they lacked evidence that she had committed any crimes. At least she was pretty sure they didn't. At any rate, their main concern was Taylor, which left her Dain. As far as she could tell, no one was watching his house. She never saw those goons pretending to live in his neighborhood, and she knew for a fact, that he didn't have a security system. She had checked just yesterday. She would lie low for a while, and take the time to plan her next move.

****

Dain opened his door to Anderson. He wondered what had happened to find him on his doorstep again. They hadn't heard a peep out of Mia in a couple of months. He just hoped that this visit had nothing to do with her resurfacing.

"What's going on Anderson? Is Taylor okay?" He had been out of the country for the last week and hadn't spoken to Taylor in the last twenty-four hours. Dain gestured for him to have a seat.

Anderson took the offered chair. "I just wanted to let you know the latest on my sister. I know that she hasn't bothered you or Taylor since your car was targeted, but she has been seen driving through Taylor's neighborhood since then." Dain parted his lips to speak but Anderson stopped him, asking him to let him finish. Dain nodded.

"She hasn't done anything more than that. I hired someone to keep an eye on Taylor, so if she tried anything, she would be stopped immediately, although I don't think you have to worry about her anymore."

"And why is that? Do you feel just because it's been a couple of months that she won't try again? Dain asked.

"No, but I feel she won't because my father and I have threatened to get the police involved if she goes near Taylor again. Dain I want you to know that we didn't just tell her for effect, we will have her arrested if she tries anything else. I don't think she would have taken me alone seriously, but when I got Rendell involved she knew that we meant business."

Dain felt relieved. He didn't believe Mia would jeopardize going to jail, just to get his attention. He hadn't known about the security detail Anderson had hired for Taylor but was glad to hear about it. He assumed Mia had gotten bored with her antics and had moved on. It had been almost two months, since her last attack. Like Anderson, he believed Mia had finally gotten the message. Now he and Taylor could live in peace.

Chapter 24

Two weeks later

Dain had come home after an overseas flight completely exhausted. Having taken a hot shower, he climbed into bed for what he considered a week's worth of sleep. He had promised to call Taylor when he arrived home, to firm up their travel plans, but he was just too tired. After he landed, he sent her a text explaining that he would call her later. But for now, he needed sleep.

Maybe she will come over, he thought yawning, although he knew that she wouldn't. She only accepted the key he had given her, to check on his place while he was out of town. That job had been his sister's, but he had given Taylor a key, hoping she would one day be there waiting for him and not just as his friend. She was the first and only woman he had given access to his home, besides his sister. Why shouldn't he? They were friends and he loved her. They had become the best of friends, something that he didn't know he was capable of being with a woman.

Taylor had made it plain that she would be a friend, but if their relationship evolved into something more, well they would just have to see. Dain smiled at this. He hoped that they would become lovers soon; maybe during the trip they would take at the end of the week. In the meantime, he was willing to wait to see how their relationship would play out.

Yawning again, he turned over onto his side, drifting off to sleep; dreaming that Taylor was in bed beside him. He could almost feel her body next to his.

Suddenly realizing that he was not dreaming, Dain's eyes snapped open. Sitting up quickly, he nearly knocked over the bedside table trying to locate the lamp. Finally locating the switch, light flooded the room, revealing it was not Taylor in bed with him, but a seductively smiling and very nude Mia Stone.

Bounding from the bed, Dain was livid. "WHAT THE HELL ARE YOU DOING IN MY BED MIA!" He shouted at her.

Not put off by his anger, Mia responded by touching herself. "Now is that any way to treat me, Dain? We're good together baby. We have something special. Didn't you feel it in New York? Don't you feel it now?" She cooed.

Reaching for a pair of sweatpants that were at the foot of his bed, Dain pulled them on and then proceeded to pull Mia from his bed by one leg.

"Get dressed and get the hell out of my house!" He commanded her, throwing her clothes at her.

"You can't sleep with me then think you can throw me away like some trash! Who the hell do you think you are? No one treats Mia Stone like this, no one!"

Angrily, Mia charged at Dain, swinging her arms wildly trying to hit him. Losing his balance, Dain tumbled onto the bed with Mia following. Maneuvering her way on top of him, she swung again trying to punch him, with him deflecting her blows with his arms. They were still wrestling around on the bed when Taylor walked into the bedroom.

Having rethought her relationship with Dain, she had shown up with a bottle of their favorite wine, to surprise him. However, the surprise was on her after she saw a completely naked Mia and a half-clothed Dain rolling around on his bed. Dropping the bottle she held with a thud, Taylor gasped at the sight, drawing both Dain and

Mia's attention. Horrified, Dain untangled himself from a smug and smiling Mia.

Taylor immediately turned away from the spectacle that was permanently burned into her memory. She headed for the front door, with Dain on her heels. He pleaded desperately for her to stop, to let him explain, but Taylor kept running until she reached her car, where he caught up with her.

"Please, please baby…listen to me. I know it sounds like a lie but it's not what you think. I can fully explain what happened here. Just come back inside and let me explain, Taylor please!"

Dain pleaded to no avail. Taylor wasn't hearing it. All she could see was him in bed with Mia. He had told her he had rebuffed Mia's advances. He had also told her he hadn't been with any women since they had started seeing each other and she had believed him. How stupid could she have been, she thought. Men like Dain didn't change. They never do.

"Let me leave Dain, just let me go." Crying Taylor pleaded with him. "I trusted you...I believed you!" She continued shaking her head.

"Do you know why I came over here tonight? I had finally made up my mind to take our relationship to the next level. After all these months, I finally trusted enough to give myself to you. You see Dain, I have fallen in love with you and I thought that you had felt the same way. But I was so wrong, wasn't I?"

Sobbing, Taylor shoved him out of her way. Not giving him a chance to respond, she hurriedly climbed into her car and sped off. Dain could only watch helplessly, replaying what she had said, repeatedly in his mind. She was in love with him. The one thing that he had been longing to hear from her.

Suddenly, remembering what had caused all of this, he marched back into his house to deal with Mia.

Having witnessed the scene outside from a window, Mia had gotten dressed and had settled herself on the sofa to wait for Dain to return to the house. She couldn't believe her luck. The scenario couldn't have gone better if she had planned it herself. Any other time she would have been furious to know that Dain had given Taylor a key to his house, but this was perfect. Mia knew she had gotten rid of Ms. Patterson once and for all. She told her father that perseverance would win out. All you had to do was keep trying and it would pay off. For her, it had paid off in spades.

Deep in thought over her victory, Mia flinched, startled by the slamming of the front door. Not knowing what to expect next, she braced herself.

Rushing to where Mia sat, Dain grabbed her roughly by an arm, jerking her up from her seat. "YOU BITCH!" He yelled inches from her face. He was mad enough to hurl her across the room. Having never hit a woman, he was finding it very difficult not to start then and there.

"You get your ass out of my house and if I ever catch you here again I will have you arrested for breaking and entering."

Taking her by the arm, Dain dragged her to the door, shoving her forcefully outside, and slamming it behind her.

Somewhat bewildered, Mia scurried down the block to her car and quickly left the neighborhood.

#

Unbeknownst to any of them, someone else had witnessed the drama that played out at Dain's house that night. After observing the incident from beginning to end, he wasn't happy; he wasn't happy at all.

#

Taylor drove around aimlessly, unsure of where she was going. She couldn't go home for fear that Dain would show up there. She eventually found herself sitting in Anderson's driveway. She had sat there sobbing for about ten minutes before she was startled by a knock on the driver's side window. Relieved that it was Anderson, she opened the door only to collapse into hysterics, unable to speak.

Anderson had gotten Taylor out of the car and into the house, with her sobbing uncontrollably. He couldn't make out anything that she was saying, so he waited until she could calm down enough to explain. He had looked her over when he brought her inside. She didn't appear to be hurt, but he knew appearances could be deceiving.

Finally, able to control her crying, Taylor told Anderson what happened. He was beyond livid. He had warned Dain about hurting Taylor. Dain had assured him that he had broken it off with Mia months ago and that he had finally seen that light when it had come to women. Anderson had given him the benefit of the doubt, believing that he was a changed man. However, here sat a heartbroken and shaken Taylor.

"Anderson, where is Paige? I don't want her to see me like this." Her eyes darted around the room while she attempted to wipe her face free of tears.

"Don't worry, no one else is here. Paige is in Arizona visiting her parents. She won't be back until the day after tomorrow."

Relieved, Taylor relaxed her tensed body.

"Do you mind if I stay here tonight?" She asked her cousin. "I don't want to see Dain. I'm afraid he may show up at my house," she explained, wiping her nose with the wad of tissues Anderson had given her.

"Of course, you know where the guest room is. I will get you some towels. And Taylor, I'm so sorry this happened." Anderson watched an emotionally beaten Taylor head to the guest room.

After making sure Taylor was settled, Anderson left to deal with Dain.

#

After throwing Mia out of his house, Dain tried calling Taylor but got no response. He was going out of his mind, trying to think how he was going to fix this. When he couldn't get Taylor on the phone, he decided to call his sister for advice. Dani told him not to do anything until she got there. It seemed like an eternity before his sister rang his doorbell.

"Now tell me what happened." Dani coaxed her brother.

Pacing the floor, Dain preceded to explain the evening's events that sent Taylor running from his house. He explained how he had come home and gotten into bed dog-tired, not realizing that someone was in the house. How he was falling asleep when he felt a body next to him in bed. He explained his outrage when he turned on the light to find Mia fully nude lying there. He dropped into a chair as he recounted what happened next. He explained the altercation with Mia, which led him to chase after a shocked Taylor only to have her leave him.

"Dani, she said that she loved me. Can you believe that? She loves, me!" He repeated pointing to himself. "What am I going to do? Tell me what can I do to make this right?"

"Oh little brother, you have gotten yourself in one hot mess," She assured him rubbing his back.

"When you first started seeing Taylor, I was worried that you would mess things up, but not like this. I thought you would turn back into your old whorish self, but I was wrong. I've watched you with her. After you confessed your love for her, I didn't worry about you anymore. But who could have predicted this?" She asked in amazement. Mia Stone was out of her mind.

"The only thing that you can do at this point is try to get her to listen to you," she suggested. "It may take some time but she may listen. Although, I can't guarantee that she will believe you. If you want, I could try talking to her on your behalf."

"No, no, I made this mess. I have to be the one to clean it up. All this could have been avoided if I had just listened to you and stayed away from Mia."

"Dani, I had no idea that I could feel this way about any woman. I love her and she may never give me the chance to tell her or show her. Damn it!"

Dani felt sorry for her brother. She tried giving him as much hope as possible, but from a woman's point of view, considering his track record, she didn't see where he had a chance. What goes around truly does come around, she thought.

****

As predicted, Dain showed up on Taylor's doorstep, ringing the doorbell and knocking franticly. He had rushed over after he talked with his sister. He was relieved when the door was finally opened, only to be surprised that it was answered by Anderson instead of Taylor. Before he could react, Anderson pulled him into the house by his collar.

"Before you hit me, please give me a chance to explain, man please!" Dain pleaded with Anderson.

As angry as Anderson was, he conceded to let Dain explain before he knocked his teeth out. Although he felt Dain had a beating coming, he was grateful that Jayden was not in town at the time. He would have thrown punches first and asked questions later. Releasing Dain's shirt, Anderson gestured towards a nearby chair.

Dropping heavily into the offered seat, Dain explained the events that led to Taylor being hurt. He repeated the tale that he told his sister, but adding the first time, that he had come home to find Mia in his bed. He explained to Anderson that was the day that he ended it with her.

"I thought that you and your father had taken care of the Mia problem. I never thought in my wildest dreams that she would show up again. I let my guard down after months of silence from her. The vandalism had completely stopped. I just assumed that you had gotten through to her. I still don't know how she got into my house." He said shaking his head.

"Look man, do you really believe that I would have given Taylor a key to my house if I was still sleeping with Mia; hell with any woman for that matter?"

Anderson listened while Dain explained waking up with a naked Mia in his bed. He listened to his explanation as to how he was only trying to fend off her blows when Taylor walked in.

No, he didn't believe that he would have given Taylor a key had he been sleeping with other women. That wasn't his style. Dain had always been upfront with the women he entertained. Besides, he agreed with Dain. He erroneously believed he and his father had solved that problem. Turning the story over in his mind, the litigator in him dissected every sentence. Anderson finally concluded that he was telling the truth. However, Taylor may not see it that way.

"Ok, Dain. I do believe you. How you're going to get Taylor to believe you is a different story. I will do all I can to help, but all in all, you are going to have to be the one to convince her."

Relieved that Anderson believed him, Dain slumped forward with barely controlled emotion. He had to make Taylor believe that he was telling the truth. He had to. He loved her too much and there was no way that he could lose her.

"You might want to start from the beginning, this time. You know, about you sleeping with Mia? If you start anywhere but there, it won't make any sense. She will for certain believe that you're lying," Anderson advised.

Knowing that he was right, Dain could only nod. He never wanted Taylor to know that he slept with Mia, but now he didn't have a choice.

Chapter 25

Mia drove back to her apartment on a high. She couldn't believe her luck. Dain may not want her now, but after he calmed down, he would see that they belonged together. She had to admit, she didn't expect him to be that angry. Well, he wasn't that angry, she lied to herself. He was taken off guard. She would not allow herself to believe that his anger was because of his feelings for Taylor. He couldn't have feelings for her. They haven't even slept together. She had monitored them long enough to know that he hadn't slept with anyone since their time in New York.

Yes, they were good together. So good that he couldn't even be with anyone but her. He would come around, she was certain of that.

Letting herself into her apartment, Mia threw her bag and keys onto a nearby table. After doing a little dance, she made her way into the kitchen to pour herself a glass of wine. Taking a sip, she moved towards her bedroom, stripping off her clothes as she walked. Mia smiled as she turned on her sound system, dancing her way into her bathroom. Choosing her favorite scented soap, she stepped into her shower, smiling as she savored the shock on Taylor's face.

"Poor baby, having to walk in and witness Dain rolling around on the bed with little ole me." She laughed while rinsing the fragrant soap from her body.

Finishing her shower, Mia shrugged into a robe and towel-drying her hair, as she walked back into her bedroom.

"Well, if it isn't my taste of honey from the wedding reception."

Mia spun around, startled by the intruder's voice. 'What's his name' from her brother's wedding reception; her sexual entertainment for that evening, was leaning against the doorjamb of her bedroom with his arms folded.

"WHAT THE HELL ARE YOU DOING HERE?" She screamed at him, stunned at finding this man in her home. Mia had never expected to see the man again, let alone discover him casually lounging in her bedroom.

Mia first noticed him sitting in the back of the church during the wedding. She had readily assumed that he was a guest of Paige's since she had never seen the man before. Later, after encountering him again in the hotel lobby, she had chatted him up after Jayden had scared away her other prospects.

He was tall, handsome, and well-dressed. The suit that he wore was tailored to him and his shoes were handmade, so she knew he wasn't a wanna-be like most of the men who were in attendance that night. He had intrigued her, but not enough to keep her mind from Dain Sinclair. Now here he was in her bedroom.

Unfazed by Mia's outrage, 'What's his name' made himself at home on her bed, amused by her stunned expression. He didn't answer right away. He wanted to enjoy her surprised appearance a little longer. He knew she was trouble the moment he met her, but he couldn't stay away. He was mesmerized by her.

He had been away serving his country when he received his cousin's wedding invitation. He hadn't been sure that he could make it, but he had. Sitting in the last pew, to not attract attention, he had arrived at Paige and Anderson's wedding shortly before the 'I do's'. He hadn't contacted his family to let them know that he was in town, and after the message that he received during the wedding, he was glad that he hadn't.

His sister always cried whenever he had to leave for duty, so when he got the message informing him that he needed to return immediately, he chose not to let them know he was home. After the wedding, he had slipped out of the church unnoticed and had only gone to the reception to deliver his gift.

However, as he was leaving, he had come across Mia Stone. They briefly exchanged small talk, before she asked if he wanted to leave to get better acquainted. He had readily agreed. It had been three years since he had been in the company of a woman outside his fellow soldiers, so he was more than willing. Normally he didn't pick up strangers, but from Anderson's previously emailed description and the resemblance that he recognized immediately, he knew that she was Anderson and Jayden's sister Mia.

Mia had followed him back to his house, where they had engaged in some intense introductions. From the start, she had taken total control of the evening, barely clearing the entryway, before she began to disrobe. He found her to be aggressive, more aggressive than the women he was accustomed to. Standing in her stilettos fully nude, she made her way into his kitchen, where she made herself at home pouring them glasses of wine. Handing one to him, she preceded him down the hallway, in search of his bedroom. Carrying her wine glass in one hand and her red dress and shoes in the other, she quickly found the room she was searching for.

Watching him undress, she slowly smiled as she inspected his gym-sculptured body. After he had removed the last article of clothing, Mia sipped from her glass before placing it on a nearby table. Tossing her dress on the room's only chair, she slowly walked over to where he stood, before dropping to her knees, to attend to his massive erection. He could only moan while her talented mouth did its work.

Not able to stand any longer, without falling to his knees, he had finally taken control of the situation. Pulling her up from her kneeling position, he picked her up and tossed her onto the bed, delighting her immensely. Before she could recover, he had spread her legs, planting his mouth firmly on her mound. Mia was enraptured, thrashing wildly on his bed, with her climaxing almost immediately. After protecting them both, he turned her over, entering her from behind. Bracing himself with one hand by gripping the bed's headboard, he moved swiftly within her, causing them to both shudder and moan.

They had spent a few hours thoroughly enjoying each other before she suddenly rose from his bed to leave. He had wanted to spend some time getting to know her, especially after their intense encounter, but she was adamant about leaving. Mia Stone had left him lying in his disheveled bed, feeling as if he had been caught in a hit-and-run accident. Now here he was sitting in her bedroom.

"So sneaking into other people's homes is only reserved for you?" He finally asked her, further enjoying her shocked expression. "I know all about your little escapades with Dain Sinclair, Ms. Stone. You have been a very busy girl."

Mia was more stunned than she had ever been in her life. How did this man know about her and Dain, and how much did he know?

Suddenly she felt lightheaded. Making her way over to her chaise, she sat down heavily. "How...?"

"How do I know? Well, that is a long story, but one I think that you will be interested in. After you left me that night, I was ready to let things go with you, but I couldn't after you decided to mess with my sister."

"Your sister? Who the hell is your sister?" Mia asked still in a state of shock.

"You need to get to know the men with whom you bed, Mia. That way you can be informed of all the players in your little melodrama. I would have stayed out of it had you not broken the windows of my sister's car," he finally enlightened her.

Mia's eyes bulged. He was Taylor's brother. "I...I didn't know..." She started.

"You didn't know because you didn't care to know. You never asked me my name that night. I hadn't realized it until after you left. I knew who you were because I had made it a point to know. I always like to know who I'm having sex with, I'm funny like that," he added sarcastically.

"I know that you're probably wondering why I'm here. One reason and that is because of Taylor. I followed you to Dain's tonight, and I watched you let yourself into his home, illegally I might add. Not knowing what would happen, I stuck around just in case you needed my help."

"But imagine my surprise when Taylor shows up a little while later. Then she comes running out of Dain's house crying. I must admit I was angry Mia, because I knew you were the cause of my sister's pain. It was confirmed when I saw you standing in the window with that smug smile on your face."

Mia hung her head. She had been caught. She wondered what he would do now. He was right, she didn't know who he was, and at the time, she didn't care. Other than his being Taylor's brother, she still didn't know his name.

"May I ask your name?" She asked embarrassed, but still defiant.

Smirking he answered her. "My name is Kylon Patterson, Colonel Kylon Patterson with the United States Air Force.

****

Taylor lay in Anderson's guest room, with tears streaming down her face. After he provided her with everything she needed, she took a long hot shower in hopes that it would make her feel better. It didn't. She found herself crying uncontrollably, sliding down to the floor of the shower stall while the water washed over her. She couldn't believe that she had fallen for Dain's lies. She trusted him. She loved him.

Finally pulling herself together, she donned an oversized T-shirt that Anderson had left for her and crawled into bed. Taylor replayed the scene of Mia and Dain repeatedly in her mind. She would never forget the image of them rolling around on that bed with a nude Mia smiling joyously.

Why did Dain have to lie about her? She would have protected her heart had she known the truth. She hurt so much. She couldn't seem to stop the flow of tears that streamed from her eyes. What was she going to do now?

Taylor thought about the good times she and Dain shared; the intimate dinners, the silly bets that they made, the walks in the park holding hands as if they were lovers. In a way, she felt that they were lovers. She believed they had loved each other's souls. The type of love that should exist before the physical. That was why she had made up her mind that she would give herself to him completely. She was certain that they loved each other, but she was wrong, oh so wrong. Dain didn't love her and now she was stuck in a world of heartache and despair. Turning over on her side Taylor cried herself to sleep.

Chapter 26

For once, after meeting a man, Mia wished she had at least gotten a name. She might have conducted herself a little differently with Taylor. She certainly wouldn't have smashed her car windows or destroyed her home.

Mia was rightly put in her place. She had been so focused on climbing into bed with Dain that she hadn't care who Kylon was. Well, that wasn't totally true. She had made it a habit of not enquiring about the names of most of her encounters because she rarely ever wanted to see them again. This time her practice had caused this little dilemma.

"Hey, how do you know about the car windows?" She suddenly asked, truly curious. "I understand you claimed to have witnessed me breaking into Dain's house, but how do you know about Taylor's car?"

"I didn't know for certain until now," Kylon informed her with a huge grin. "You confirmed it by not denying it. Anderson told me what happened to Taylor's car. I couldn't imagine who would want to hurt her that way. But after observing you tonight, I knew I had suspected the correct person."

"So how long have you been following me?" Mia was beginning to feel the heat and wondered if he had enough evidence to cause her some serious trouble; like in some jail time trouble.

"Me personally, this was the first time."

"What do you mean by you personally?" Mia did not like where this was heading.

"After your window-bashing party, I hired a private investigator to follow my sister. I wanted to know exactly who might be out to hurt her. Imagine my surprise when I received an email with a photo of you coming out of Taylor's house, hence leading me to believe that you were the one who vandalized her car."

"I followed you tonight because I wanted to confront you about my sister and I wanted to see you again. I would have come sooner, but after our night together, I had to return to duty the following day. So, I had to wait until I could return stateside to track you down. I was just about to leave my car to knock on your door when you pulled out of your driveway, so I followed you."

Kylon didn't know what made him follow Mia, but he was glad that he had. After tailing her to her destination, he observed her leaving her car and walking a block up the street. Curious to see what she was up to, he followed her and parked across the street from the house she approached. He watched her walk around to the side of the house, raise a window, and climb inside. He hadn't known what to make of this until Dain Sinclair pulled into his garage.

Thinking that she may need help of some kind, he waited. He wanted to know why Mia was sneaking into Dain's house again. Kylon knew his sister was seeing Dain, and like Anderson, he didn't like it, but she was an adult. Taylor had initially claimed she and Dain were only friends; that was until recently. She had confided in him that she had feelings for Dain and wanted their relationship to go further.

So watching Mia climb through Dain's window had him troubled; not to mention all the videos and other evidence that had been compiled on her. Mia's behavior reeked of more problems for his sister. It also appeared that Dain might not be aware of Mia's presence inside his house because of her method of entry.

Kylon watched Dain emerge from the garage to check his mailbox before retracing his steps, letting his garage door down. Kylon waited, not sure what would happen next. He didn't have to wait long before he spotted Taylor pulling into the driveway. She exited the car carrying takeout bags along with a bottle of wine.

Watching his sister let herself into Dain's home with a key, Kylon had an uneasy feeling that things were about to heat up, and not in a good way. With Mia sneaking into the house and now Taylor arriving, he wanted to do something, but he didn't know what. While trying to come up with a solution, he heard Dain shouting for Taylor to wait. Moments later his sister burst from the house heading for her car in tears. Seconds later, a partially clad Dain tore from the house in pursuit, trying to get her to stop and talk to him. Kylon watched him plead with her to listen, telling her that he could explain what happened.

Kylon's first reaction was to exit his car and help his sister. With Dain only wearing jogging pants, with no shirt or shoes, he wondered if Taylor had caught them in the act. That was before he witnessed the devious grin that spread across Mia's face as she watched the scene from a nearby window. He wondered then if Mia had set them up. And from all appearances, he believed she had.

Instead of leaving to follow his sister, Kylon waited to see how the drama would play out. Moments after Dain returned to the house, slamming the door behind him, Mia was forcefully removed. He watched a not-so-smug Mia hurry down the block to her car. He had his answer.

Following Mia back to her place, he waited before letting himself into her home. He heard her in the shower and she sounded pretty pleased with herself. He waited in another room until she came back into her bedroom where he confronted her. He knew that he should be angry with her, for what she had put his sister through, but at the same time, he was aroused.

Since meeting Mia and sharing that night with her, he hadn't been able to forget her. He knew she was bad for him, considering the way she had seduced him and left without caring to know who he was, but she captivated him. He wanted to know her, and not just intimately but personably.

Kylon had come to a crossroads. Now that he had all the answers, what was he going to do with the information?

As if reading his mind, Mia asked, "So what now? Are you going to tell your sister?"

"That depends," he replied. "Dain wants to be with Taylor and you have to respect and accept that."

Mia wasn't sure that she agreed. She still wanted Dain and wasn't certain if she could stop trying to convince him they belonged together. But then again, after eyeing this striking man sitting on her bed, she suddenly wanted him, at least for now. Mia let her eyes roam over Kylon's jean-clad thighs, remembering what lay between them.

"What if I won't accept that?" She asked, still weighing her options.

"Then we have a problem. A problem that I'm sure you wouldn't want the police to know of."

Mia raised a perfectly arched brow at hearing this. She certainly didn't want this to turn into a legal issue. Sure, she had destroyed some things, but surely her actions weren't enough to involve the police. During her pursuit of Dain, she never once gave thought that her actions could land her in jail.

"Did I fail to mention, while you were being followed by the investigator that he digitally documented your escapades through photos and video?" He asked with a raised brow of his own.

Mia realized she had no leverage here. If she didn't comply with Kylon's wishes she could be in serious trouble. She had no choice but to end her campaign to win Dain. Mia also understood if Kylon wanted her punished, he wouldn't be in her home revealing all of his evidence, she would be sitting in a jail cell instead. And if he didn't want her arrested, what did he want? She thought she knew the answer.

Rising from her chair, Mia untied her robe, letting it fall to the floor. Padding across the room to stand in front of him, she reached for the hem of his shirt, pulling it over his head. With this accomplished, Kylon pulled her to him, as he fell back onto the bed with her landing on top of him. He kissed her feverishly.

Moaning, Mia unbuckled his belt, before undoing his zipper while they continued to explore each other's mouths. Breaking the kiss, Kylon freed himself from his jeans and underwear. Reaching into his pocket, he retrieved a condom, which he quickly donned, plunging into Mia soon after. His skin tingled with the sensation of being inside her. He watched as her face displayed the pleasure that she was receiving. In too deep, to stop, literally and figuratively, he would have to straighten out this mess with his sister later.

#

Mia awoke smiling and well-satisfied. What's his name…Kylon had loved her thoroughly throughout the night. Rolling over to tell him so, she found the space empty. She looked to where she had last seen his clothes, only to find them missing as well. "Touché," she said with a smile.

Chapter 27

Taylor was grateful Anderson allowed her to take a few days off of work. She didn't think that she could be effective in the condition that she was in. She lay across her bed flipping from one channel to another with her remote control. Nothing on television seemed to interest her. Giving up, she switched off the television and tossed the remote onto the floor.

She couldn't believe Dain was sleeping with Mia. She should have known there had to be more to the vandalism other than Mia throwing a tantrum because she couldn't have her way. She wondered how long they had been sleeping together. Had Dain been with Mia all along?

Shaking her head, Taylor sat up and looked at her reflection in the mirror across the room. Her hair was disheveled. Her eyes were swollen. She looked a mess. Deciding that she had grieved over this tragedy long enough, she climbed off the bed and headed for the shower.

Letting the warm water flow over her knotted shoulders, her mind wandered back to Dain. She loved him. That was the hard truth. She loved a man who could never love her. She thought about the time they spent together after Mia trashed her house. He was so kind, so giving. Was that all an act? She remembered how she wished he would kiss her, whenever they were lounging on the couch watching movies or when she tried to teach him to Salsa. He never did. She had assumed he was keeping his promise to be a friend. Now she knew it was because he was sleeping with Mia. Why would he want to settle for the taste of a simple kiss, if he could get the whole plate from Mia?

Mia Stone, a spoiled brat if she ever saw one. What could he possibly see in a woman who made it her business to sleep around? She had that woman-child pegged from the beginning. She wasn't fooled by her innocent act as Jayden had been. She saw Mia for the man-eater that she was.

Mia was a few years younger than Taylor and a couple of dress sizes smaller, but Taylor had never let her size or age diminish her worth. It wasn't as if she were ready for a rocking chair, she was only thirty-four. As for her size, at five eleven she was a healthy and quite curvy size twelve. Not every man wanted a size two woman. At least she hadn't thought that Dain had disapproved of her size. He was always hugging her or placing his hands on her hips when they danced together. Maybe he did prefer the skinny petite type, Mia's type.

Sighing, Taylor knew that she would have to talk to Dain sooner or later. She preferred later, much later, but if she wanted answers and closure, she would have to choose sooner. As if confirming her thoughts, her doorbell chimed. She wondered if it was Dain. He had come by a few times and she had refused to answer his pleas to open the door. Sighing again, she donned a robe and made her way to the door, deciding that she would let him in this time.

Preparing herself for Dain, Taylor opened her door to her brother. Smiling brightly, she flung herself into Kylon's arms.

"What are you doing here? When did you get back?" Taylor asked as she pulled him inside.

"To answer your first question, I'm here to see my sister, and to answer your last; I got back a couple of days ago," Kylon told her.

"A couple of days ago? Why are you just now dropping by?" Taylor questioned him with her hands folded on her hips. She was ready to tear into him for not visiting her sooner.

Ruffling her hair as he did when they were children, he explained. "I had a few things that I needed to take care of when I got back into town. But I'm here now, doesn't that count?" He laughed at her folded arms and skeptical expression.

"Well, I guess I'll let you slide, this time." She smirked, unfolding her arms to hug her brother again. "Are you hungry? I can cook up something quick."

"No, I'm good. Here come sit with me." Kylon pulled her towards the sofa. "I came by to see how you were doing. I've talked to Anderson, so I know what's been going on. How are you doing Taylor?"

Taylor's smile faulted and then faded. She dropped her head under her brother's scrutiny. She wondered just how much did Kylon know about the situation between her and Dain. Taylor opened her mouth to speak but was cut off by Kylon.

"Before you enlighten me, I just want you to know that I know the whole story," he told her, sensing that she was about to minimize the situation.

Taylor rolled her eyes. She had forgotten how Kylon was able to read her mind. When they were kids, she would try to skirt around the severity of a situation only to have him call her on it.

"Kylon I feel like a fool. Granted I only planned to befriend Dain and not get emotionally involved but I am. We'd been spending so much time together; getting closer. I thought he felt the same way. At least, I thought that he was heading that way. I was wrong."

Shaking her head, she continued. "Technically, we weren't together and he had never made me any promises, but he told me he wasn't sleeping with Mia, but he was. What am I going to do?"

Kylon hugged his sister, kissing the top of her head. "The first thing that you need to do is hear his side of the story."

Taylor looked up at him then, puzzled.

"Hey, at least hear the man out. You may find what he has to say enlightening."

Sitting up and folding her arms again, Taylor inspected her brother closely. "Where is my brother and what have you done with him?" She asked jokingly.

"Kylon are you feeling ok? Any other time, you would have marched right over to Dain's and whooped him silly. What gives?"

"Sis, I have learned over the years that there are always two sides to every story. Do you remember that old saying, believe half of what you see? Tell me, what type of woman is Mia?" He asked as if he didn't know.

"She's a selfish little tramp that would do anything to get what she wants." Taylor rolled off the description without hesitation.

"Ouch, just say what you feel." He chuckled at her description.

"Well you asked me what type of woman she is, and that is what I see. I knew what type she was the first time that I met her."

"Now think about what you just said. Do you think that she is capable of making you believe the worst in what you saw? In the time that you two spent together, had Dain given you any indication that he was seeing Mia?"

Taylor thought over his questions. Out of all the times that she was with Dain, except for the first time that they had dinner together, there hadn't been any women present in his life other than his sister Dani. No phone calls or people dropping by. She turned these things over in her mind.

Finding her voice, she finally responded. "No, but he could have decided to hook up with her that day, Kylon." Taylor pointed out.

"Do you really believe Dain would have given you a key to his home if he planned on entertaining Mia, knowing that you could drop by anytime? The man may be an ass. Your words not mine," Kylon interjected when Taylor raised her hand to object.

"The man isn't stupid, Taylor nor do I see him wanting to hurt you for any reason."

Taylor thought about this. True, Dain may be many things but cruel is not one of them.

"What motive would he have for hurting you like that?" Kylon continued as if reading her mind. "And didn't you tell me, when he gave you the key, he asked you to use it freely?" Making his case, Kylon waited for her answer.

Kylon was right. Dain did say it wasn't what it seemed. Why would he give her a key to his home only to have women traipsing in and out? It didn't make sense.

Letting out a long cleansing breath, Taylor agreed with Kylon. "You're right, it doesn't make sense. Oh Kylon, what have I done?" Taylor exclaimed placing her hands on top of her head.

"I don't know what you have done, but I know what you should do. You should...." He started.

"Yeah, yeah, yeah. Look stay as long as you like and let yourself out." Taylor leaped from the couch, heading for her bedroom to change. She had work to do.

Grinning, Kylon got up to let himself out. His work there was done.

"Now to go deal with Miss Mia Stone," he said as he headed to his car.

#

Dain was dog-tired. He had flown a turnaround trip to Los Angeles. Normally he would still have the energy to dance the night away if he chose to, but not tonight. He credited his fatigue to his less-than-peaceful nights. Since Taylor left, he hadn't slept much. He had tried several times to talk to her, but she wouldn't accept his calls or answer her door.

Anderson had recommended that he give her some time. He was confident that she would come around. Dain wasn't so sure. Looking back on that night, he could see how incriminating the scene with Mia had been. If the roles were reversed, he would have had a difficult time believing the truth himself.

Letting himself into his house, he immediately became alert. There were candles lit throughout his home, with soft music playing from somewhere within the house. There were vases of roses everywhere with a path of petals leading through the kitchen and down the hallway to his bedroom.

Dain was furious. Mia was back in his house. Taking off his jacket, he removed his tie and rolled up his sleeves. He was going to get rid of her once and for all. If he had to call the police, so be it.

Marching down the hallway, kicking rose petals as he stepped, he burst into his bedroom ready to do battle with Mia Stone. Dain came to a complete stop when he saw who was in his bed this time. It was a scantily clad Taylor. Believing that he was imagining things, he squeezed his eyes shut, certain that when he opened them it would be Mia in his bed, not Taylor. He was more tired than he thought. However, when he opened them he still saw Taylor.

"You aren't seeing things Dain, it's me," she assured him.

Taylor, after speaking with her brother, left her house with a plan. She had made a huge mistake in not letting Dain explain things. She made several stops along the way to his house. First, she stopped at a florist to purchase the roses and candles. Next, she stopped at the nearest mall to shop for lingerie, something that she hoped he would like. Lastly, she picked up champagne and chocolate-covered strawberries. She had called Dani before she left, to find out when Dain was due back into town. She thanked her lucky stars that he was due that night. Knowing that she had little time before he arrived home, she executed her plan quickly. Letting herself in with the key he had given her, she prepared the house and herself for his return.

She had donned the hot pink teddy that she bought earlier, along with matching hot pink kitten-heeled slippers, with fluffy puffs of fur on top. She lit candles and placed them strategically around the house. She put the champagne on ice and the strawberries on a silver tray she found in the kitchen. Finding a preset music list on his system, Taylor pushed play and waited.

Speechless, Dain walked further into the room as Taylor sat up patting the space beside her, indicating for him to sit. Obeying her command, he sat down next to her, not knowing what to say, but glad she was there.

"Taylor what...how...?" He stammered.

Placing her palms on either side of his face, she pulled him to her, kissing him softly.

"I had time to think about what happened and came to the conclusion that I needed to let you explain. I realized that the situation didn't make sense. There had to be a logical explanation," she answered. "So I am ready to listen."

"Taylor, I need to start from the beginning. Something I should have done in the first place. Anderson told me that I should have told you the whole story the first time, but I didn't listen. If I had, maybe the whole Mia thing wouldn't have happened in the first place." Dain looked into Taylor's expectant face and pressed forward.

"It all started at Anderson and Paige's wedding reception. "You have to remember I was a different guy back then. Please keep that in mind." Taylor nodded. "I had spotted Mia and tried to get with her that night, but Dani stopped me. That's when I encountered you in the lobby." Taylor raised an eyebrow but said nothing.

"Later she showed up on one of my flights to New York and we hooked up then." Dain watched Taylor close her eyes but motioned for him to continue.

"The weirdest part about that encounter was the entire time that I was with her, your face kept appearing in my mind and that was before you and I had gone for coffee. That was the reason why I urged you to come with me. I realized that I had made a terrible mistake in sleeping with Mia. I had gone to the party to see you. So I was mighty glad when I encountered you coming up the walkway.

"There were so many things that I wanted to say to you that night, but didn't have a clue how to start. So I thought I would just show you instead by the way I interacted with you. I was beyond thrilled when you agreed to be my friend, at least that was a start."

"But getting back to Mia. Dani stopped me from ending it with her that night at the dinner party. It was a hookup that I regretted and I wanted to end it with her as soon as I possibly could. But she had other ideas. I came home from work one day and found her naked in my house. I told her to get dressed and that it was over between us. I thought she had accepted things until your car was vandalized. That is why Anderson and I suspected her. The rest of what I told you at your office was the truth. I had rebuffed her and she retaliated."

"So how did she get into your house? What was going on the night that I walked in on you?" Taylor was awestruck by the lengths this woman would go to get what she wanted.

"I found out how, after the last time she was here, the night you found us. She had pried open a window at the back of the house. I discovered the tool marks after I threw her out. And to answer your question about what happened,

I had come home and gone to bed, only to wake up to find Mia had slipped into bed beside me naked. When I rejected her this time, she tried to fight me. We fell on the bed and that is when you walked in."

"Taylor, I know that I should have told you from the beginning that I slept with Mia, but I didn't want to look any worse in your eyes than I already had. Can you forgive me?" Dain looked into Taylor's eyes, praying that she wouldn't get up and leave him a second time.

"Dain, I can't fault you for something that you did in the past, before us." He visibly sighed with relief. "But, if you ever lie to me again, even by omission, there will be hell to pay. Do you hear me?"

Dain grabbed her then, kissing her passionately.

"I promise that it will never happen again." He kissed her again. "Now let's talk about this outfit."

Rising from the bed, Dain pulled Taylor to her feet. He whistled as he slowly turned her, admiring her skimpy lingerie.

"Simply beautifully."

Pulling him to her, Taylor continued kissing him. She began helping him out of his shirt, while he kicked out of his shoes. She helped him with his pants, letting him strip off the rest.

"Can you wait just a few more minutes while I jump into the shower? I want to wash the day's work off of me."

Nodding her agreement, Taylor let her eyes travel over his muscular body as he retreated to the shower. She poured each of them a glass of champagne while she waited for him to return.

Dain showered in record time. He couldn't believe Taylor was in his home, in his bed waiting for him. Quickly brushing his teeth, he emerged from the bathroom wearing a towel around his slim waist. He found Taylor lounging seductively on his bed, offering him a glass of champagne.

After taking a sip, Dain placed both of their glasses on the nightstand. "Now where were we?" He asked before he laid her back on the bed.

Dain kissed her hungrily, delighting in her soft moans. He inhaled the feminine fragrance that she wore, loving its intoxicating scent. His gaze moved to the breasts that he had admired from day one. Sliding the straps of her teddy from her shoulders, he proceeded to remove it from her body to access those breasts. Kissing one then the other, he enjoyed the reaction that he drew from her.

Not to be outdone, Taylor pulled Dain's mouth back to hers, as she gently pushed him onto his back. Straddling him, she kissed his chest, moving south to the top of the towel that covered his growing gift to her. Reaching for the towel to remove it, Taylor found herself once again lying under Dain, minus his towel.

He wanted to let her have her way, but he couldn't wait to join them together. Reaching into a drawer on the nightstand, Dain retrieved a condom. He quickly applied the protection before he ripped the teddy's matching panties from an aroused Taylor.

"I will buy you many more," he promised before lowering his mouth to hers. Still kissing her, Dain plunged inside of Taylor, nearly losing control from the feel of her body wrapping tightly around his shaft. They both cried out in the pleasure that their connection brought.

Dain had to steady himself before he could move inside of her. He had waited for months to show her what he felt for her, he wasn't about to lose control now. Finding his bearings, he slowly began to thrust inside of her, finding his rhythm. Taylor moved with him feeling the pressure rise inside of her. Dain picked up the tempo as he felt the heat rise between them. Moving faster, he reveled in the pleasure he witnessed in Taylor's features. This is the woman he needed, he thought and he would never let her go. Moving even faster, Dain held onto her as they both climaxed.

Barely able to catch his breath, Dain fell back onto the bed, bringing Taylor with him. After a while, he was able to find his voice. He kissed her, pulling her closer to him.

"I'm in love with you too, Taylor Patterson."

Chapter 28

Kylon knew his sister would go ballistic if she knew he was seeing Mia. He was sure that Anderson and Jayden would have something to say as well. Kylon never thought in a million years that he would fall for his cousins' sister. He was shocked when Anderson emailed him about encountering Mia with his father Rendell. He was just as surprised as the rest of the family about his uncle's other family.

He remembered when Rendell left Adaisha and Anderson. His parents were always discussing what a low life Adaisha had married, leaving a pregnant wife and child behind. He and Anderson were only months apart in age and had grown up together. They were more like brothers than cousins. They shared everything, toys, baseball cards even secrets. So when Anderson confided in him about his rage against Rendell, he understood.

After the brothers met Mia, Anderson told him about Jayden's obsession with protecting their little sister. Anderson on the other hand didn't view Mia as Jayden had. He saw her as a full-grown, capable woman. Kylon totally agreed with Anderson. Mia was more than capable. He wondered what Anderson would do if he found out that he had been sleeping with his capable sister.

"I don't think that he would approve," Kylon mumbled before knocking on Mia's door.

"I didn't think that you were coming back," Mia told him once Kylon was inside. She hadn't heard from him in a couple of days. She thought he had ghosted her as payback her for his sister.

"I was cleaning up your mess," he told her, before pulling her into his arms. "I hope that you're finished with your mayhem, now that you've been caught."

"I won't bother Dain or your sister again if that is what you're referring to. How can I, with all the evidence you have against me? What do you plan to do with it anyway?" She asked genuinely concerned.

"If you promise to never bother them again, I will destroy it. If not...well," he teased her

"And if I agree, do I have to admit to them what I've done?" Despite everything she had done, Mia dreaded having to have that conversation with either of them.

"Let me see. Since things have been resolved between Dain and my sister, I don't see why you have to admit anything. Although, I would be good if sometime in the future after everything calms down, you could maybe, I don't know, send them a peace offering?"

"Well, in that case, you can destroy it. I promise to leave your sister and Dain alone for good. Now that I've done this for you, what are you going to do for me?" Mia asked with a knowing grin.

"Let me show you," Kylon said, picking her up in his arms to carry her to bed.

#

"I have to fly to D.C. tomorrow, so I won't be around for a couple of weeks." Kylon was holding Mia in his arms after they had made love.

"Tomorrow? But you've only been here a few days." Disappointed Mia sighed.

She was beginning to care for this man. Something that she hadn't done before with any man, not even Dain. Feelings were never a part of her game plan. She thrived off of loving them and leaving them. Somehow, Kylon had set up camp in her heart and she didn't like it. Maybe it was for the best that he was leaving. While he was gone, she could reel in her emotions.

"No worries my love, I will return."

Kylon didn't tell her, but his assignment in Washington would be his last one. He was retiring from the Air Force. Too many tours in war-torn countries had taken its toll. It was time that he got out before he became burnt out. Besides, he wanted a family and hopefully, he could have one with her.

"I think we should let our families know that we're seeing each other when I get back. I know we'll catch grief from both sides, but I don't care. I like you Mia Stone and I enjoy spending time with you and I want everyone to know that."

Mia didn't answer, but only smiled when Kylon suggested this absurd plan. If she had her way, that was never going to happen. Even if she was inclined to give in to her growing feelings, there was no way either of their families would accept them as a couple and she couldn't blame them. Kylon had a good heart, but she didn't think she deserved him.

Yes, she would spend their time apart to come up with a way to extinguish their so-called relationship.

Chapter 29

Tor Hudson was elated to be done with his last assignment. He didn't know if he could have followed Mia Stone much longer without turning her in to the police. He just hoped Kylon Patterson knew what he was doing because the woman was certifiably crazy. Tor knew women could get fanatical when their boyfriends or husbands cheated, but this woman had no right to act out. The man she obsessed over wasn't hers to begin with.

The job may not have been to his liking, but he was pleased, after depositing the generous check Kylon had given him. In addition to his fees, he had added a hefty bonus for a job well done. Tor would be able to open his business now instead of later, thanks to Mia Stone and her antics. He had already purchased a suite of offices near the river. The property had cost him a pretty penny, but he found it to be a good investment if he wanted to attract a more upscale clientele.

Besides location, Tor knew presentation was everything when it came to a successful business, so understood the need to have his offices professionally designed. Not knowing much about these things, he had off-handedly mentioned his need to Anderson, who had recommended his wife's firm, *Beautiful Colors Designs*. After the purchase of the building, Tor made an appointment with the design firm to get the ball rolling. He wanted to open as soon as possible.

Tor had crossed paths with Anderson, in locating the whereabouts of his father, Rendell. After learning of the family connection, he couldn't believe Mia and Anderson were related.

Leaving his newly purchased office space, Tor checked his watch and realized that he was about to be late for his appointment if he didn't get a move on.

#

"Andee, has my next appointment arrived yet?" Dani asked over the phone.

"No, not yet, but he still has a few more minutes to spare," Andee answered.

She checked the appointment time again, noting that Dani's next appointment had eight minutes before he was counted tardy. Something that Dani deplored. She had always been a stickler when it came to company time.

Personally, Andee thought she was a little too uptight about it. Stuff happens. Along with the appointment time, Andee checked the man's name again, Tor Hudson.

"I wonder what a Tor looks like," she whispered to herself with a chuckle. As if on cue, the door swooshed open bringing him inside.

Stalking towards Andee's desk while she looked on, Tor took in the appearance of the woman eyeing him, with interest. He noted her smooth mocha skin, her large clear brown eyes, framed by long thick lashes, along with her naturally spiraled curls. Tor was instantly fascinated.

Andee was equally impressed with what she saw. The man was divine. He was tall, his body slim but athletically built. His brown wavy hair perfectly complimented his reddish-brown skin. She guessed that he had Native American or Hispanic heritage floating around his otherwise African DNA.

Andee inwardly shivered as his piercing gaze pinned her to her chair. Realizing that she was staring, she mentally shook herself, breaking the spell he had cast on her.

"May I help you?" She asked this intriguing stranger.

Reaching Andee's desk, Tor responded, never taking his eyes from hers. "Yes, Tor Hudson. I have an appointment with Dani Sinclair.

So this is what a Tor looks like, Andee surmised. "Good afternoon Mr. Hudson, I'm Andee Dalton," she responded, offering him her hand.

Tor, grasping her hand firmly, felt a slight quiver emitting from her. He smiled.

Coming out of her trance a second time, Andee withdrew her hand and offered him a seat, while she retreated to Dani's office.

"Hey did my appointment show up yet?" Dani asked while flipping through some documents she would need for her appointment. Not receiving a response from Andee, she looked up to find her back pressed against the wall, wide-eyed.

"What's wrong with you?" Dani asked her.

"To answer your question, yes, your appointment is here," she choked out.

"So what's the problem?" Dani asked her again with growing concern.

"I... I don't know," Andee truthfully answered; still wide-eyed with disbelief. "The man walked into the office and I lost my mind. I feel all funny inside. I don't know what to make of it," she further explained, hugging herself.

Dropping the pen she was holding, Dani rolled her eyes and stood to walk around her desk. The man couldn't be all that, she thought.

"Come on, let me see who has you all tied up in knots."

Taking her by the arm, Dani led Andee back to the lobby. When they entered the reception area, Tor stood as Dani moved forward to introduce herself. It wasn't lost on either of them that Andee had quickly retreated into Paige's office.

"Hi Mr. Hudson, I'm Dani," she greeted him with a firm handshake. "If you will come with me to my office, we can get started."

When Tor accepted Dani's hand, he noted the resemblance to Dain immediately. This had to be Sinclair's sister, he gathered. He had followed the man enough to remember what he looked like.

Following Dani to her office, Tor glanced over his shoulder, hoping to catch a glimpse of Andee, but she was still inside Paige's office. Maybe I'll see her before I leave, he thought. He wanted to know more about Ms. Andee Dalton.

#

"Is there something that I can do for you, Andee?" Paige asked her as she came rushing into her office and closing the door behind her. Paige studied her, wondering what had her all worked up. She just hoped that there wasn't more trouble on the horizon. They had more than enough with Mia.

"Have you ever met someone who captured your whole being's attention the moment you laid eyes on them?" Andee asked.

Not knowing where this was coming from, Paige decided to ask what was going on before she attempted to answer her question.

"You want to enlighten me as to what you're talking about?" Paige was fully aware this was unlike Andee.

Taking this as an invitation, Andee took a seat at Paige's desk. "Paige I just met the most incredible man. He seemed to touch my spirit when he looked at me. That has never happened to me before. Granted the man is good looking and I have met good-looking before. Hell Jayden is gorgeous, but this transcends looks. I can't explain it. It's like he touched my soul with his eyes."

Paige leaned forward to study Andee. Her interest was piqued by her strange assessment of this mystery man. Paige had never heard her speak this way about man, and certainly not Jayden. And speaking of Jayden, she wanted to know where he stood within this assessment of this new man.

"Who are you speaking of?" Paige asked, eager to learn the answer. She noticed Andee appeared to be awe-struck.

"Dani's current appointment, Tor Hudson. He just walked in here and I couldn't think. It may sound crazy, but I feel as if a part of myself just came walking into the lobby." Shaking her head, Andee looked to Paige for answers.

#

Meanwhile, in Dani's office, Tor was only half listening to her explain the details of the design process. His mind was in the other office with Andee. He'd met and had women before, but this woman was something different. He couldn't quite put his finger on what set her apart. He felt the need to explore this undiscovered territory more. He just hoped she wasn't married. If she was married, he would drop it immediately. He never encroached on another man's territory. If there wasn't a ring, then all was fair, and may the best man win.

"Excuse me," Tor interrupted Dani, during her explanation of color schemes. "Not to change the subject and we will continue with designs, but could you tell me if Andee is married?" Tor boldly asked Dani.

Leaning back into her chair, Dani assessed the situation. Not only does Andee have the hots for this guy, but he has a good one for her. She could see why Andee found him interesting. He was extremely handsome, but so was Jayden. It has to be something only these two get, she surmised. At any rate, it wasn't her place to judge. Considering Andee and Jayden had been seeing each other for a year, they seemed to have hit a wall in their relationship. Besides they weren't married to each other, so what the hay. She just wanted Andee to be happy, with whomever that may be.

"No, Andee isn't married," she finally answered him with a barely perceptible smile. Dani was amused. Oh, Jayden, this man is going to give you a run for your money, she thought.

Pleased with the answer, Tor motioned for her to proceed with the pitch, although he would agree to anything. It didn't matter what it cost to get his offices up and running, his mind was in overdrive as to how to win the lovely Andee Dalton.

#

"So, the man just stopped you in the middle of your spiel, to ask if Andee was married?" Paige was asking Dani, while Andee looked on. Dani nodded in the affirmative.

"Wow, he didn't waste any time."

"What did he say to you before he left?" Dani asked a stunned Andee.

"He just said that he would be seeing me again," she said with a shrug. She didn't know exactly what that meant but she found herself shamefully eager to find out.

"Well, I'm sure you'll be hearing from him again. The man's body may have been in the meeting with me, but his mind was definitely out here with you," Dani remarked. "I don't think he cared what I was saying. He would have agreed to anything, as long as he could see you again," she added, equally intrigued by Tor's interest in Andee.

"And from the reaction that she had to him, I'm sure she won't mind seeing him again either. Which brings me to the next question," Paige added, turning to Andee.

"Don't say it. I know. What about Jayden? I never said that I was dumping Jayden...jeez. I just made a few comments about the way the man made me feel that's all. And I'm sure the feeling will pass. Mr. Tor Hudson just caught me off guard. I'm with Jayden, end of discussion."

"You may be dating Jayden, but you aren't married to him. You know what my mother used to say, if you're not married, you're still considered single. And you my dear do not have a ring on that finger yet," Dani reminded her.

Andee bit her lower lip. She was in trouble. She just hoped that she could handle it and not mess up what she had with Jayden. She loved Jayden...didn't she? But if she loved him, why had another man captivated her so easily?

#

Tor left *Beautiful Colors*, deep in thought. So the lovely Andee was single. Although Dani didn't come out and say it, her pause led him to suspect that Andee was somewhat attached. An attachment he could work with. He just hoped the man in question could handle the loss, because he meant to have Andee. He had found his soul mate.

Chapter 30

"I take it from that smile that you and Dain have made up?" Anderson asked Taylor. They were in his office wrapping up the day's paperwork and going over his notes on an upcoming trial.

"Yes. After talking to Kylon and listening to your advice, I realized that what I walked in on that night didn't ring true. Although, Dain should have told me from the get-go that he slept with Mia. I would have known how to handle that situation."

"WHAT THE HELL DO YOU MEAN, DAIN SLEPT WITH MIA?" Jayden had walked into his brother's office catching the end of their conversation.

Taylor and Anderson's attention immediately turned to Jayden who was more than displeased at what he just heard. Anderson quickly spoke, hoping to defuse the explosive situation.

"Hey little brother, I didn't know you were in town,"

"And from what I'm hearing it's a good thing too. Now what is this about Dain sleeping with Mia?" Jayden asked again, not about to change the subject until he got to the bottom of this debacle.

Recognizing that this was her cue to leave, Taylor stood to retreat to her desk; hoping to leave the brothers to work this mess out alone.

"It's great to see you cousin, but I will just—" she began, only to have Jayden cut her off.

"Oh, no you don't. From what I just heard, you are a part of this and I want to know everything." He told Taylor, pointing to the seat she had just vacated, indicating that she should sit back down.

Looking to Anderson for help, but not getting any, Taylor returned to her seat.

"Jayden, calm down, and let's discuss this rationally," Anderson pleaded.

"Rationally? How can I be rational, when our sister is sleeping with that sleazy bastard Dain? You know what type of person he is Anderson. He's bad news." Jayden was furious.

"He's not the same person he was before, Jayden. He's changed," Taylor tried reasoning with him.

"How can you defend him? Are you sleeping with that low-life bastard too?" He asked her in disbelief.

"Jayden! Stop it!" Anderson shouted. "Taylor, you go on home. I'll take care of this."

Not waiting to be told twice, Taylor grabbed her notebook and hurried from his office, closing the door firmly behind her, before Jayden turned on her again.

"Now sit down, shut up, and listen!." Anderson ordered his brother. He waited for Jayden to take a seat before he continued.

"Yes, Dain and Mia slept together once months ago. And before you start ranting again, these are consenting adults we're talking about. You have no right to stick your nose in another adult's bedroom business. So get over it!"

Jayden said nothing. He sat there huffing, still angry.

Jayden was quiet for a long while before he spoke. "So, are you going to tell me what's been going on or not?"

He had to admit Anderson had a point, but it didn't excuse why he was just now hearing about his sister and Dain.

Anderson took a long drawn breath, expelling it before he plunged head-on into the saga of Mia, Dain, and Taylor. He knew that Jayden wouldn't be happy, but he hoped by the end of his tale, Jayden would have some insight into the real Mia and not the innocent little sister he made her out to be.

Anderson emphasized the point to Jayden that Mia was the one who pursued Dain. He told him about her showing up on his flight to New York, where their sister and Dain did indeed have sex. He explained how Dain recognized his mistake, and broke it off with Mia.

Jayden's eyes widened when he heard about the destructive things that Mia had done, once she discovered Dain and Taylor were seeing each other. Anderson gave him all the brutal details, from Mia smashing Taylor's car windows to her climbing into bed with a sleeping Dain, causing Taylor to flee from Dain's house in tears. Once Anderson had finished, Jayden was overwhelmed.

"So Mia did all of those things?" Anderson nodded. "Wow, I guess you're right, we really don't know this girl.

Anderson, I heard everything that you said, but how do you know that Dain has really changed and won't hurt Taylor? She deserves the best."

"Jayden, once again, whatever happens between those two is their business. But to answer your question, I do believe he has changed. Dain loves Taylor and wouldn't do anything to hurt her. You have to let grown folks handle their own business, Bro."

Nodding, Jayden had one last question. "So tell me. Who knew about all this?"

"Everyone knew except you. I felt it was best to leave you in the dark until I got this sorted mess under control," Anderson admitted.

"So Andee knew, and she said nothing to me?" Jayden was growing angry again. How could Andee not tell him, when it involved his family?

"Don't blame Andee; I thought it was best that she not tell you," He explained.

"Well, no offense my brother, but Andee isn't dating you. Her loyalty should have been to me not you."

Jayden was irritated. He had been back and forth visiting Andee for months and she never said a word to him.

Clenching his jaw in full-blown anger, Jayden rose to his feet. "I will see you later. I need to see Andee," He threw over his shoulder as he flung open the door. Jayden stalked out of Anderson's office on a mission.

"Jayden wait! Don't blame her, it was my call!" He shouted after his brother. Jayden didn't stop.

"Damn it!" Anderson immediately picked up the phone to call Andee. He didn't want Jayden to blindside her.

"Paige...where is Andee?" He asked his wife after she answered the office phone.

"She's gone for the day...Anderson, what's wrong?" Paige was alarmed by the worry she heard in his voice.

"The short of it is, Jayden knows everything and he is angry and aiming for Andee. Let me see if I can catch her at home or on her cell. I'll see you later at home."

Anderson hung up from Paige to dial Andee's cell. It went straight to voicemail. Trying her home number, there was no answer. Anderson swiped his hand down his face. He wondered what would happen if he couldn't warn Andee. He just hoped that their relationship could survive this.

#

"You look worried," Dani commented after Paige hung up.

"I am worried. It seems that Jayden is in town and knows of the mess that has been playing out between Dain, Mia, and Taylor. And from what I gather, he knows Andee knew and kept it from him. He's angry Dani, angry with Andee."

"Oh no. This is not good," Dani lamented. She was quiet for a moment before speaking again.

"Paige, what are the odds that on the same day, Andee meets Tor Hudson that Jayden would come to town gunning for her? Looks like a case of one door closing and another one opening to me," Dani speculated. Somehow she didn't think this was a coincidence.

"You know, I was thinking the same. I have a bad feeling that their relationship won't survive this. You know how Jayden feels about honesty. I admit, at the time, I didn't think keeping all this from him would be a problem because we were all keeping the secret, not just Andee."

"Yeah, but we aren't the ones he's dating. He trusted Andee." Shaking her head, Dani added, "Whatever happens, we'll be there for her."

"Yes, we will," Paige agreed.

****

Andee was about to answer her phone when her doorbell rang. Looking at the phone's display, she saw the call was coming from Anderson's office. Assuming that it was Taylor calling, she made a mental note to call her back later. Looking through her peephole, she smiled when she saw that it was Jayden. Throwing the door open, Andee threw herself at Jayden, happy to see him.

"Hey baby, what a surprise! I didn't know you were coming. I could have picked you up from the airport," She said grinning.

"I wanted to surprise you," Jayden told her, closing the door. He followed her into the living room, where she offered him refreshments. He declined.

"Baby, what's wrong?" Andee asked him, concerned that he was frowning.

"I just left Anderson's and imagine my surprise, when I overheard him and Taylor discussing what's been going on for months right under my nose."

Andee was relieved that he finally knew, but that was about to be short-lived. "I am glad that you finally know. It was hell keeping that from you," she admitted.

"That's just the point, Andee. *You* shouldn't have kept it from me. Of all the people who knew what was going on with Dain, Taylor, and my sister, *you* should have told me!"

Andee was taken aback at his anger. "Are you blaming me for this Jayden?" She asked him with some anger of her own.

"Yes, I'm blaming you! If you had told me from the start, I could have stopped Mia from making a fool of herself!" He shouted.

"I don't believe this! How can you say that, Jayden, huh, how? Mia is a grown-ass woman, knowing right from wrong just like the rest of us mortals. How were any of us to know she would turn out to be bat-shit crazy? She is not the demi-god you've made her out to be!" She screamed back at him.

Andee calling his sister names made Jayden angrier. "Is that what you think of Mia, some crazed lunatic?" He asked, clenching his teeth in disbelief.

"What else would you call her? Who breaks out car windows and sneaks into people's homes trashing them, just because a man didn't want her, uh? Who does that other than someone crazy as a loon? If you weren't so busy cock blocking, maybe you could see the type of person your sister really is!" Andee couldn't believe that he was blaming her for his deranged sister's actions.

"You know what Andee? I often wondered if we would last, but now I have my answer. If you think my sister is nuts, I can only imagine what you really think about me! I want you out of my life. We're done! I don't ever want to see you again!" Jayden all but pushed the words into her face.

Having had his say, Jayden turned on his heels and stomped out, leaving Andee standing in the middle of the room with her jaw hanging. She jumped at the slamming of her door.

Stunned, Andee screamed, "What the hell just happened!" She closed her eyes as she tried to grasp what had just taken place.

"Oh my God, he's gone." Realization kicked in and she began to cry.

The phone rang again. Thinking that it was Jayden calling to apologize, Andee quickly answered it.

"Hello?" She asked barely above a whisper.

"Oh, Andee thank goodness. It's Anderson. Jayden knows about Mia and Dain. I wanted to give you a heads up so you wouldn't be caught off guard."

"Too late," Andee said before hanging up.

Chapter 31

Andee sat on a park bench watching the ducks glide on the water, trying to make some sense of what happened between her and Jayden. She couldn't understand how he could blame her for his psycho-sister's actions. She had been sitting there for a couple of hours ignoring her ringing cell phone. She didn't want to talk to anyone. Every time she thought the tears had stopped, more showed up to prove her wrong.

Sighing, she threw the last of the bread she brought to the waiting ducks. She was so deep in thought that she hadn't noticed that someone had joined her on the bench.

"If he makes you cry like that, he isn't the man for you," the stranger said suddenly.

Andee jumped, startled at the sound of the man's voice. She had to shield her eyes from the sun to make out who was speaking to her. It was Tor Hudson.

"Are you following me?" She asked, surprised to see him there.

"No, I'm not following you. I was walking my dog when I spotted you sitting here wiping away tears."

Andee leaned forward to see where he pointed to his dog. She saw a German Sheppard tied to a bike rack.

Wiping away the last of her tears, Andee looked a Tor. "I guess I must look a sight, sitting here boohooing like an idiot?" She asked him clearly embarrassed.

"You're not an idiot. The man who made you cry is the idiot. You are a beautiful woman who deserves a man who will make you smile not cry," Tor informed her.

"So I guess now you're going to tell me that you're that man, uh?" She asked him amused.

"Why, yes Andee Dalton, I am that man," he boldly answered her.

****

"Were you able to reach Andee?" Anderson asked his wife.

"No, and I'm worried about her. What else did she say when you talked to her?" She asked him again.

"Nothing more than what I told you. She said it was too late and hung up."

Anderson sighed. "This is entirely my fault. I should have never asked her to keep secrets from Jayden. I should have just told him the truth and let the chips fall where they may."

"Don't beat yourself up over it. We still don't know what happened. It may not be as bad as we think."

Although Paige tried to reassure her husband, she wasn't so certain herself. She hoped everything was ok with Andee and Jayden, but she feared the opposite. If only she could just hear from Andee. The doorbell rang as she was pondering Andee's well-being.

"I'll get it."

Anderson rose to answer the door. Paige sighed with relief, sure that it was Andee. Her relief was short-lived when Jayden walked into the room.

"Jayden, where is Andee?" She asked him.

"I don't know and certainly don't care," he replied.

Paige's shoulders slumped at hearing this bit of news. "What happened, Jayden?" She tried again.

"I broke it off. We're done."

Anderson and Paige looked at each other in stunned disbelief.

****

Andee was stunned by Tor's reply. She hadn't really expected him to answer her question, let alone be so serious about it. At first, she thought he might be joking until she searched his unsmiling face. He isn't joking. Who is this man?

Tor watched the myriad of questions play across Andee's face. He knew she was wondering if he was real. He had never been as serious as he was at that moment. He wanted Andee to be a part of his life. He knew that the moment he met her. The trick was to get her to go along with his plan. Tor finally smiled as he imagined the possibilities of convincing her.

"You're serious, aren't you? Andee asked him, accepting the determined look in his eyes.

"Yes, I am. Do you have a problem with that?" He asked her, fully expecting an answer. He observed her as she turned the question over in her mind. He knew she wanted to explore the possibility. He watched her question herself. Asking if she should really take a chance on him.

"Mr. Hudson, probably for the first time in my life, I don't know what to say," she admitted.

Andee thought back to earlier that day when she first met Tor Hudson. She recalled how her body and mind had responded to this stranger. How for a split second, she had wanted to give in to his spirit's calling. Never one to act on impulse, she felt the urge to give in again, at that very moment.

"A simple yes or no will be sufficient," Tor nudged her. He knew that it seemed as if he were pushing her, but he didn't believe in wasting time. Especially when it came to something so important.

Andee looked into Tor's eyes, examining the seriousness of the moment. Stepping out of her comfort zone, she answered him.

"No, I don't have a problem with it. But there is one thing that I have to know first. How did come to possess the name Tor?" She asked with a smile.

Tor smiled at her acceptance of their destiny.

****

"What do you mean you broke it off?" Anderson asked his brother. He couldn't believe what he was hearing.

"I can't trust her. She should have told me what was going on. There is no excuse for what she did," Jayden informed them.

"Jayden I told you, I'm the one responsible for you not knowing, not Andee," Anderson reiterated. Out of the corner of his eye, he watched his wife pick up the phone and take it into the other room.

"As I told you, she wasn't sleeping with you. Besides, she thinks Mia is a nut job. If she feels that way about our sister, what does she really think about me?"

Anderson couldn't believe what he was hearing. He wanted to shake some sense into his brother. How could he be this foolish?

"I want you to really think about what you're doing. Are you really going to lose a good relationship, because you were left out of the loop on something that was none of your business to begin with?"

"Look, I don't want to talk about this anymore with you or anyone else. It's over and that's all there is to it," Jayden told his brother. "I had better get to the airport to catch my flight home."

"Before you go, there is something else you need to know. I was trying to tell you earlier before you blew out of my office. I went to Rendell about Mia. I figured with her behavior, I needed some help in dealing with the situation. He knows her best."

At this new information, Jayden was livid. "You mean to tell me that you went to our bastard of a father for help instead of me?" He asked, pointing at himself. "Has everyone gone crazy? How could you go to him and not ask me to help, Anderson?"

"As I just stated Jayden, our father knows her better than we do! He is the only person who can handle Mia. What would you have done if I had come to you, huh? I would really like to know."

"First of all, I would have made sure Dain Sinclair stayed away from her. The key was with him. If he would have kept his paws off of her, none of this would be happening!"

"Did you not hear what I told you earlier? Mia pursued him, not the other way around. Anyway, that is beside the point. It doesn't matter who pursued whom. Mia did not have the right to do those things she did, under any circumstances. Your answer is why I couldn't enlist your help."

"You know what man? I can't handle this right now. I'm out of here!" Anderson watched his brother leave his home.

Hearing the door slam, Paige reentered the room. She heard most of the brother's discussion and knew Jayden was making a huge mistake, one he would regret deeply.

"Were you able to get in touch with Andee?" Anderson asked, hoping that she had.

"No. Her phone keeps going straight to voice mail."

"I called Dani. She is going to meet me at Andee's place. Anderson, I'm really worried about her. It's not like her to not answer her phone no matter what's going on."

"Go. Let me know if you and Dani need my help."

Anderson kissed his wife. He hoped she and Dani were able to find her. Shaking his head at his brother's self-righteousness, Anderson knew Jayden would live to regret his haste decision.

Chapter 32

Andee unlocked her front door and stepped over the threshold of her home with Tor and his dog Smoky in tow. Deciding that they needed to explore their earlier conversation further, she invited him back to her place.

"Would you like something to eat? I was about to make dinner before...well before everything went to hell," she explained with a frown.

"Only if you let me help," Tor answered.

"It's a deal if you tell me about your unusual name," Andee offered, as she led the way to her kitchen to start their meal.

Commanding Smoky to stay put, Tor followed.

Washing his hands at the kitchen sink, while Andee pulled ingredients from the refrigerator and cabinets, Tor explained. "My name in Hebrew means 'king' and in old Scandinavian, it means 'thunder'. My mother was obsessed with old and unique names. She was looking for a name that was strong and regal, so for her, Tor fit the bill," He added with a small smile.

"You know, Andee isn't exactly a common name for a woman," Tor countered.

Laughing, Andee thought about it. "You're right. I guess we have something in common there. My mother is a big fan of unusual names also. She told me that she was determined to name her baby girl Andee regardless of what anyone else thought. However, she spelled mine with two E's instead of a Y or IE," She added with a shrug of a shoulder.

"Tell me, why you were crying earlier?" Tor asked suddenly; changing the subject and the mood in the room.

Frowning, Andee thought about what he was asking. For a brief moment, she had forgotten about Jayden.

Sighing, she spoke. "The man I have been seeing for the past year broke it off with me today because I chose to mind my own business and not report to him the affairs of others. One of the people being his psycho sister," Andee added with attitude.

She went on to explain the ends and outs of the relationship between Dain and Mia, which led to the breakup. Although Andee only used first names, she was unaware that Tor was more than familiar with the players in that particular saga.

"You're kidding right?" He asked her, while they each performed their task in preparing their meal.

Andee shook her head, indicating that she was not kidding. She wished that she had been.

Wow, the man is a bigger fool than I thought. Tor marveled at Jayden's stupidity.

To Andee, "You were right, that was neither your business nor his. Does he make it a habit of getting into other people's affairs?"

"When it comes to his sister, whom he has only known a few months, I might add, he can't see her for who she really is. The girl is a menace to society."

"Sounds like it."

Tor agreed wholeheartedly, but could not tell her that he knew firsthand what a nut job Mia Stone is. It wouldn't be ethical. With what he just learned, Tor shook his head. He marveled at the chain of events that led him to Andee. Who knew that surveilling Mia Stone would bring this wonderful woman into his life? Something great came out of that job after all.

Although he was sorry Andee had gotten hurt in the melee, he was glad that her man, that is ex-man, was a fool. Tor was determined to make sure Jayden Stone remained an ex.

The ringing of the doorbell grabbed their attention. Tor just hoped that it wasn't the boyfriend coming to apologize before he had a chance to make Andee forget him.

Andee excused herself to answer the door, asking Tor to watch the cooking food. He did what he was asked, keeping his eyes on the food, but his ears were tuned to the other room.

Andee took her time answering the bell. Part of her wanted it to be Jayden on the other side of that door, but another part of her had accepted Tor. Pulling the door open, Andee was relieved to see Paige and Dani.

"Why aren't you answering your phone?" Paige asked her while she pulled her into a tight hug. "We were so worried about you."

Dani took her turn to hug Andee. She felt some guilt about her predicament. It was her brother's whorish ways, which caused all of this mess.

"Honey, how are you doing? Jayden told Paige and Anderson that he broke things off with you. I am so sorry," she told Andee. "I feel responsible for Dain's part in this."

"This isn't your fault or Dain's," Andee reassured her.

"I can't believe he would break up with you over Mia's foolishness. That was a bit extreme," Dani continued.

"I agree," Tor said from the doorway of the kitchen, drawing the women's attention.

Hearing his master's voice, Smoky came from behind a chair where he was lounging, startling both Dani and Paige.

"The food is done," Tor informed Andee while patting Smoky's head.

Both of Andee's guests turned to her for an explanation.

"It's a long story," she told them, looking as if she had been caught with her hand in the cookie jar. "Anyway, you two are welcome to join us for dinner. There is more than enough."

Dani and Paige looked at each other and then at Tor, both declining simultaneously, stating that they would let them get back to their meal. They let Andee know that they would talk to her later. Paige and Dani were leaving with more questions than answers.

"Well, what the hell was going on there?" Dani asked Paige who was equally perplexed by the presence of Tor Hudson. "That man didn't waste any time moving right on in as Jayden let himself out," she added with wonder.

"I can't wait to hear the explanation for this one," Paige muttered as she got into her car.

#

"I'm pretty sure that your friends are dying to know how I came to be in your home, after just meeting me," Tor said with a chuckle. He was setting the table for dinner.

Tor was relieved that it wasn't Jayden Stone at the door, although he was more than ready to deal with him had the opportunity presented itself. Any man who would leave Andee the way that man had, didn't deserve her. Jayden was out and Tor was going to make damn sure he stayed out, by showing Andee what a real man was capable of.

"I am more than certain that I will get the third degree later," she replied, placing the prepared food on the table.

#

Anderson was working on a brief when his wife returned. He raised his head when she walked into his home office.

"Well that was quick, did you find her?" He asked Paige refocusing on his paper.

"Oh yes we found her and how," Paige answered him cryptically.

Hearing the inflection in her voice, Anderson raised his head yet again from his work. "What's going on?" He asked her, noticing the smirk on her face. "Did my knot-head brother come to his senses and was there apologizing?" Anderson asked, sure that must be it. He assumed that she and Dani had interrupted Andee and Jayden's making-up.

"Not even close," she answered, further drawing Anderson's attention.

"When we got there, Andee wasn't alone though. Dani's new client was there with his dog, cooking dinner." She told him with a widening grin. She enjoyed the puzzled expression on her husband's face.

"Care to elaborate?" Anderson placed his pen on the desk, very interested now.

"Well to make a long story short. A new client came into the office today that had Andee tied into a knot. And it seems that she had the same effect on him. During his meeting with Dani, he had asked, if Andee was married. So whom do we find having dinner at Andee's? Tor Hudson."

Anderson's eyes widened at this disclosure. "Tor Hudson? Tall guy, athletically built, with close-cropped brown wavy hair? Anderson.

Paige nodded.

"Well, well, well, what a small world. That was an unexpected plot twist."

#

Jayden took a long swallow of his beer as he ran through the channels on the television. He didn't know why he bothered to turn it on. Nothing could satisfy him tonight. He had been ignoring calls from Anderson since he got home. He would talk to him eventually, but not tonight. He couldn't believe that Anderson turned to Rendell of all people to help him. But the biggest kicker of the day was Andee's betrayal.

He couldn't understand how she could keep something so important from him. She was his girl. He should have been able to trust her if no one else. Although he was angry with his brother for keeping Mia's escapades from him, he knew that eventually Anderson would tell him, when he found it necessary. However, Andee hadn't planned to tell him at all. She would have just let Anderson carry the whole weight. He wondered what else had she been keeping from him.

Finally turning off the television, Jayden drained the last of the beer from the bottle. He felt confident with his decision to break it off with her. If he couldn't trust her now, how could he trust her in the future? Closing the door on that chapter of his life, he got up to get himself another bottle of beer.

Chapter 33

"You've been quiet all evening, what's wrong?" Dain asked Taylor. They had just gotten back from dinner and were lounging at her place.

"Jayden overheard Anderson and I talking about the Mia mess and he took it out on Andee," she informed him.

"Andee? What does Andee have to do with Mia's crazy ass?" Dain was completely confused with his line of logic.

"He blames Andee for not telling him about you and Mia. He feels that she deliberately betrayed him. Can you believe that?"

Dain shook his head in the negative.

"But that isn't the worst of it," she continued. "He broke things off with her."

Dain stared at Taylor in disbelief. "What is wrong with that idiot? And why does he have this obsession with defending Mia? She is an adult who can make life choices without anyone's help. It's not like she hasn't been doing that for years before he and Anderson came on the scene."

"Paige thinks, psychologically, that Jayden is protecting Mia from men like Rendell. Jayden witnessed the hurt and struggle of his mother and somehow he feels as if he needs to protect Mia from the same fate," Taylor explained.

"By the way, he has an arsenal of anger for you too, so I would stay out of his path for a while."

"I can handle Jayden, but I sort of feel responsible for what Andee must be going through. She really liked that guy. I have always thought of her as a sister, you know? We grew up together, so I feel the need to whoop Jayden's ass for hurting her like that. Especially over something, that wasn't even his business. If he wants to blame anyone he needs to start with his psycho sister."

Taylor nodded her agreement.

Turning his attention back to Taylor, Dain kissed her. He had something else in mind that he knew she would agree with. Making his way from her lips to her neck, he placed her hand on his growing erection. He wanted her to feel what he was thinking. He was just about to strip her bare when the doorbell chimed. Taylor made a move to answer it.

"Leave it. If we ignore it, maybe they will go away," he told her with a lust-filled voice. He tried again by unbuttoning her blouse, only to have the intruder ring the bell multiple times in quick succession. Sighing, Dain gave up when Taylor stood to get the door, buttoning her blouse as she walked.

"Maybe they have the wrong address," he mumbled disappointed. Hearing Taylor greet her brother, Dain quickly grabbed one of her throw pillows to cover his bulging erection. He already had one woman's brother after him; he didn't care to make it two.

"Come on in and meet Dain." He heard her say.

Trying to look anyway but aroused, Dain sat up straighter, still clutching the pillow to the front of his jeans.

"Dain I want you to meet my brother Kylon," Taylor informed him when she re-entered the room with Kylon in tow.

Shaking Kylon's hand, but not attempting to get up, Dain caught Kylon's furrowed brow, as he took in the pillow on his lap.

"So we finally meet," Kylon said with a smirk, letting him know he was busted. "Anderson and my sister have told me much about you," Kylon continued.

Inwardly Dain groaned. Will he have to defend himself from another brother?

As if reading his thoughts, Kylon added. "Don't worry man, I believe in minding my own business," He assured him.

Dain visibly relaxed.

"In that case, it's good to meet you. I've heard a lot about you also. Taylor is very proud of her big brother. She brags about you all the time. I understand that you're military," Dain stated.

"Yes, Air Force...which is what brings me here tonight. I know this is going to make my sister very happy."

Turning towards Taylor, Kylon continued with his news. "In about two weeks I will be officially retired from the Air Force."

Taylor squealed her joy. She never liked the fact that he was stationed in war zones.

"Oh, I am so happy." Taylor grabbed her brother in a tight hug. "So when did you decide to do this?" She asked, releasing him.

"Well, I've been thinking about it for a while. The harshness of war has finally taken its toll on me. Sis, I've had enough. I'm leaving for D. C. in the morning for the last phase of my departure from the military."

Kylon thought that he would wait until he got back to tell her the other reason why he decided to leave, Mia Stone. It was for the best. He didn't want to spend the rest of the night defending his position in their relationship.

"So what have you decided to do once you retire?" Dain asked.

"That I haven't quite decided yet. I have a few things rolling around in my head."

One of those things he wanted to do was be a husband to Mia. Apart from that, he was unsure. He had saved and invested his money wisely, making it possible for him to retire completely, if he chose to do so. However, one thing was for certain above all else, he wanted to give Mia emotional security, something that he felt she lacked.

"I am going to enjoy having you around more often. I have been so frightened, knowing that you were in harm's way day in and day out." Taylor hugged he brother again. "I have missed you so much."

Kylon smiled at his sister. Now she wouldn't have to cry each time he left for duty. "Well, that's why I came by, to give you the good news."

Turning towards Dain, he spoke directly to him. "Now, I will leave you two to continue doing whatever it was you were doing before I arrived," he said, while he hugged his sister again.

"It was good to finally meet you, Dain. And I am sure that I don't have to tell you to be good to my sister," he added.

"No, you don't. You can count on that," Dain agreed.

"Let me walk you to the door." She was so happy with the news.

Relieved that Taylor's brother wasn't after his head, Dain patiently waited for her to return, so he could finish undressing her.

Chapter 34

"So, you ready to tell us how Tor Hudson happened to be at your home yesterday, cooking dinner?"

Paige couldn't wait to interrogate Andee when there was a lull in office activity. She, Dani, and Andee were gathered in Paige's office enjoying a late lunch.

Andee was amused by her friends' barely contained curiosity. They had been chomping at the bit all day. However, because of all the phone interruptions and appointments, they weren't able to question her about Tor until now.

"It's quite simple," she told them deliberately milking the moment. "After Jayden stormed out, I felt stifled by being inside my house, so I went to the park to feed the birds and think. Oh, and by the way, I'm sorry for not answering your calls; I wasn't in the mood to talk to anyone," she interjected.

"Yeah, yeah, yeah we understand, so get to the good part and stop stalling," Dani told her growing impatient.

Laughing, Andee continued. "I was feeding the birds.."

"You've already said that, now get on with it." This time Paige interrupted.

"Ok, no more stalling. "I was sitting there feeling sorry for myself when Tor sits down beside me. He had been in the park walking his dog when he spotted me sitting there wiping away tears, so came over to comfort me. He explained to me that I didn't need a man who would make me cry, but I needed someone who would make me smile. He told me that I needed him," she told them with a smile, as she remembered the moment.

"Anyway, we were having such a pleasant time talking, that I invited him and Smoky over for dinner, end of story."

"No, that's not the end of the story. What happened after we left?" Dani wanted to know.

"Well, we had a little dinner, some wine, and just talked. I learned what his name meant and how he came about it. I also learned that he wants to spend time with me and I agreed," she added shrugging a shoulder. "I like him. I like him more than I should; I might add."

"Why do you say that? If you like the man, you like the man, period," Dani scolded, with Paige nodding her agreement.

"Jayden and I were in a relationship. I have no business getting involved with Tor on the very day Jayden dumps me," she reminded them.

Paige shook her head. "Andee, you're human, not to mention that you're attracted to the man. You're no longer in a relationship, so now you have the opportunity to explore that attraction. Besides, Jayden's loss can be a better man's gain. Don't get me wrong, I think my brother-in-law is a great person, but he made a foolish move."

"I agree with Paige," Dani added. "If it was that easy for Jayden to dump you, I say go for it with Tor. He may be the one for you. And, please don't take what I'm about to say the wrong way, but Andee, I do believe you love Jayden. However, I don't think that you are in love with him, nor is he with you. I know what 'in love' looks like and Sis, you just didn't have that glow with Jayden."

"The only thing that I have to add to that is follow your heart. If Tor is the one to make you happy, then you should go with that," Paige advised.

"So what else did you learn about Mr. Hudson?" Dani asked.

"Tor is a private investigator, who wants to start his own small business," Andee informed her. "But I guess that's why he was in the office yesterday. Did he tell you that?" She asked Dani, who nodded.

"Oh, oh, I almost forgot," Paige interjected. "Anderson knows Tor. He does some investigative work for him from time to time. He was the one who recommended our firm for his office designs. So, Andee, I guess you owe my husband for bringing him here."

"Wow, this city is too small. What are the chances of that happening?" Dani asked.

"Not to change the subject, but have you heard from Jayden?" Paige asked Andee.

"Not a word," she replied, and she wasn't worried that she hadn't, thanks to Tor.

Chapter 35

Two Weeks Later

"I am so happy for my brother," Taylor was telling Andee, Paige and Dani. They were preparing food at Taylor's for Kylon's retirement party. Taylor was so happy that he was finally retiring that she insisted on throwing him a party. She had invited family and friends, all who were happy to share in the joyous occasion.

"Andee, did you invite Tor?" Dani asked, munching on a homemade tortilla chip.

She smiled. "Yes, I did. We have been spending quite a bit of time together. I didn't know that I could be this happy with anyone other than Jayden, but Tor has been like a dream come true for me."

Andee gushed whenever she spoke of Tor. She knew that she was wanted in Tor Hudson's life. She felt that want each time they were together. She found him to be a very passionate man when it came to displaying his feelings, something that she never experienced with Jayden. Andee thought she would miss the man she had spent the past year with, but she didn't. Tor made sure of that.

"Oh my goodness Andee, I'm so sorry. With all that's happened, I forgot," Taylor apologized with a puckered brow.

"You forgot what?" She asked her perplexed.

"I invited Jayden to come to the party. I am so sorry." Taylor felt bad about the blunder on her end.

"Taylor, how could you not invite him? He's yours and Kylon's cousin. I would have been surprised if you hadn't invited him," Andee reassured her with a shrug. "It's not a problem. Besides, with all of our close ties with being friends and relatives, Tor and I know that we would have to face him eventually."

"Have you heard from him since you two broke up?" Paige asked her.

Neither she nor Anderson had heard much from Jayden since the breakup, but Adaisha assured them that he was well.

"No I haven't; not one phone call," she told them shaking her head. "I guess you can say that he is truly done with me."

'You know, at first, I was hurt beyond belief, but after Tor showed up, he made me aware of some things that were lacking in my relationship with Jayden. I really thought that I was happy before, but ladies this man that I am with now is incredible! He speaks to my soul."

"Does that mean that you have gotten to know him Biblically?" Dani asked, curious.

Andee shook her head. "We're getting to know each other from the inside out, becoming friends before we become lovers. Who knows, we may wait until after we're married to take that step," Andee confided with the group.

"Married?" Have you two been talking about marriage already?" Taylor asked while she removed her dish from the oven. She was just as surprised as the rest of the group.

"Yes we have discussed it and it's a very good possibility, one that I can't explain. It's as if you know when you find that person that is meant for you. You just know it without hesitation. It's like Dani said, I loved Jayden, but I wasn't in love with him, and my only regret is that I gave my body to him."

Andee's friends all spoke at once concerning this last confession, wanting to know what she meant.

"Ladies please, let me explain."

Dani, Taylor, and Paige quieted to let Andee continue, each eager to learn what she had to say.

"Each of you knows how I come off as someone who is super confident. Someone who wears her femininity with pride. But what you all may not know is my view on sex. I've only had a couple of sexual partners in my life. Sure, I've dated, but that was all they were just dates. I have always viewed sex as something special, something that should be shared with the love of your life. I thought that was Jayden and I was wrong. I believe if I had taken more time to get to know him before jumping into bed with him, I would have discovered that he was not the one."

The others looked at one another, never knowing this about Andee.

"The good thing about Tor is that he understands and fully accepts my point of view, which makes him more endearing to me. I don't want to sleep with another man that is not my husband."

She looked at each of them before she spoke again. "Ladies, whether we want to admit it or not, sex takes a toll on our spirits as well as our bodies, when we let someone inside of us who is not meant for us. I don't want to put myself in that position again. So, that's why we're waiting." She ended her confession with a shrug.

There she said it. She just hoped that her friends didn't view her as some sort of freak of nature. She hadn't meant to get so deep into the subject, but this was who she was and she wouldn't change for anything in the world.

"Wow," Taylor responded quietly. She had never thought about sex the way that Andee just described it. It is supposed to be special, but she never could have put it in the perspective that Andee just summed up.

"Wow is right. Andee out of the four of us, I would never have described you as the most profound one. That was beautiful and enlightening Sis. Why hadn't you ever spoken like this before?" Dani asked in amazement.

"It had never come up before. Even though we have all had our relationship wins and fails, we have never gotten into a deep discussion about the bones of those relationships," she stated.

"Andee..." Paige was in awe of her friend. "...you are so right. If we as women would stop to think about how we place ourselves in relationships, our lives and our relationships would be one hundred percent better." Going to her, Paige hugged her, finding a new respect and admiration for her lifelong friend.

"Ladies, I hate to break this up, but we only have a couple of hours before our guests and the guest of honor will be arriving, so let's get cracking," Taylor informed.

The women had returned to their assigned tasks when the doorbell rang.

"Who can that be this early?" Paige asked looking at her watch. They still had a little over two hours before the guests arrived.

"I'll get it," Taylor told the group.

The others continued their food preparation until they were interrupted by Anderson's arrival.

"Anderson, what's wrong?" Paige asked her husband when he entered the kitchen wearing a troubled expression.

Not answering Paige, Anderson turned to Taylor. "What time was Kylon's flight due to arrive?" He asked his cousin.

"At six fifteen, he's coming here straight from the airport. Anderson, what's going on?" She stared at Anderson with growing unease.

Instead of answering her question, Anderson asked her another. "What was the flight number Taylor, do you recall?"

Everyone in the room was alarmed now. The same question was on everyone's tongue. Taylor was the only one to verbalize it.

"1420, Anderson, tell me what's going on." She was near hysterics at this point. By this time, the doorbell chimed again. Andee left to answer it.

Taking Taylor into his arms, Anderson broke the news to the room. "I am so sorry, but flight 1420 out of D.C. crashed on its way here. There were no survivors."

Taylor was stunned, while Dani and Paige gasped in disbelief. Andee reentered the kitchen with Dain, Tor, and

Devin in tow. They too had heard about the crash and had rushed over to Taylor's.

"It can't be his plane!" Taylor shouted with indignation. "He is retired from the Air Force. He told me so this morning when I talked to him. He told me that he would see me soon." She told the group as she pulled out of Anderson's embrace. Dain took his place, trying to comfort her.

"Dain, my brother was not on that plane, do you hear me!" Dain just nodded as he held her, hurting for her.

With the chime of the doorbell, Taylor collapsed in disbelief and grief. Dain had to hold her up to keep her from falling to the floor.

The doorbell continued to chime repeatedly, bringing more people to Taylor, trying to offer her some comfort. Adaisha and Matthew arrived with Adaisha in tears for her nephew and niece. More friends and family arrived offering their condolences.

Dain had taken Taylor into her bedroom trying to calm her to no avail. She couldn't accept that Kylon had come so far to die now. He had done several tours in war-torn countries without a scratch, so there was no way that he had come home to perish, could he?

#

Mia sat outside of Taylor's house in her car, weeping bitterly. She had spent the time Kylon was away, trying to distance her heart from him. She thought that she had succeeded until she turned on the television to learn that his flight had crashed with no survivors. She had lost it. He had called her that morning to let her know what time he would be back in town. He had asked her to meet him at his sister's house for the party because he would be coming there straight from the airport. He wanted her there because they were to tell everyone that they were together.

Mia had not intended to be at Kylon's party, because she didn't want to be with Kylon or so she had tried to convince herself. That was before she had turned on the news to the crash of flight 1420. She thought that she would pass out from the news bulletin informing the viewing audience that the plane's impact had killed everyone on board. Mia realized then that she loved Kylon Patterson, and had spent the time he was in D.C. trying to distance herself from that truth. She had broken down in tears at the news that he was gone; never getting the chance to tell him how she felt.

Mia remained in her car feeling regret for all the drama that she had caused Dain and Taylor. All the time that she had wasted with them, she could have been spending that time with Kylon. Not knowing what else to do, she found herself sitting outside of Taylor's house, wanting desperately to go inside to be with the people who loved him.

Knowing full well that she may be stopped at the door, Mia got out of her car. She needed to be there, even if no one believed that she knew Kylon, let alone loved him. She quietly let herself into Taylor's house. She stood by the door unnoticed as she observed the grief that had gripped the room. She didn't see Taylor, but she wanted to find her to share her grief.

Spotting Mia, Anderson excused himself from his mother and wife to speak with her. "Mia, what are you doing here? This is not a good time; we just found out that Taylor's brother died in a plane crash. Taylor does not need to see you here. She's going through enough."

Mia was just about to explain why she was there, when Taylor came out of her bedroom enraged when she saw Mia, drawing everyone's attention.

"What the hell are you doing here Mia? Have you come to make more trouble for us? Don't you think that my brother's dying is enough, without you adding more pain to the mix?" Taylor couldn't believe that this bitch would show up at her home.

Mia burst into tears. No one knew what to make of this. Anderson took her by the arm to lead her out, only to be stopped by the door being opened from the outside.

It was Kylon. The room burst into pandemonium. There were tears of joy and a multitude of questions, all being asked at once. Anderson saw this as his opportunity, to remove Mia from the house, but he was stopped by Kylon.

After everyone had calmed down, relieved that it was indeed Kylon and not an apparition, he pulled Mia to his side. This gesture raised more than a few eyebrows, including Anderson's and Taylor's.

"Let me explain. First off, I took an earlier flight from D.C. I got in this morning exhausted, so I decided to turn off my phone to get some sleep before the party. I had no idea that my original flight had crashed until I got into the car and turned on the radio. When I heard the news, I raced right over, because I knew you all would think that I was gone. But as you can see, I am alive and well." Kylon took the edge off the moment by bowing, which brought laughter and relief.

"Second, this lady is not going anywhere," he said of Mia.

He pulled her into his arms and kissed her passionately, drawing gasps from the crowded room, especially from Taylor, and Dani. Mia was so relieved that Kylon was alive that she didn't care who witnessed them.

"I love her, I love this woman," Kylon informed the room after he reluctantly broke off the kiss. "And if I am correct by that smile on her face, she loves me." Mia nodded before kissing him again.

"Will someone tell us what the hell is going on?" Dain asked. He among some of the others wanted to know as well.

Kylon explained meeting Mia, on the night of Anderson and Paige's wedding and some of the events that transpired afterward. He told how he and Mia had connected and had become close. He didn't reveal all of the details to the group but decided that he and Mia would explain to Dain and Taylor later, hoping that they would forgive a misguided Mia.

"So, you were hired to follow Mia," Andee stated to Tor after Kylon had pulled her aside to explain Tor's role in Mia's mess.

Kylon was quite surprised to find him there with Andee and felt that he had to come clean about hiring Tor. He didn't want there to be any friction between them, especially after learning what happened with her and Jayden.

Tor opened his mouth to explain why he didn't tell her, but she silenced him.

"You don't have to explain. I know that your client's information is confidential." And to prove her understanding, Andee pulled him to her for a long slow kiss.

Meanwhile, Taylor was in the kitchen with Dain, Kylon, and Mia, questioning Kylon's sanity and choice of women.

"How could you be involved with the woman who destroyed my car and home, not to mention tried to cause trouble between me and Dain?"

Dain was silent, letting Taylor handle her brother.

Before Kylon could speak, Mia spoke up. "Taylor, I want to apologize to you and Dain for my behavior. I was more than out of line for the things that I've done and I am deeply ashamed."

Taking Kylon's hand, she continued. "Your brother has shown me that I can be loved without degrading myself or by being a brat because I didn't get something that I wanted. I thought that I had lost him today. I thought that I had lost my chance at real love. I have been given a second chance and there is no way that I am going to mess that up."

Mia looked up at Kylon with love in her eyes, something that Taylor recognized, as she felt the same for Dain.

"Taylor, I hope that you and Dain can forgive Mia someday. I know that it won't be easy considering all that has happened." Kylon spoke. He understood it was a lot to take in considering that everyone thought he died, and now here he was explaining his feelings for his sister's archenemy.

"I guess I have to forgive her." Dain chimed in. "She isn't the only one to blame for what happened. Before Taylor, I used women for my gain, never thinking about the consequences. I took what I wanted without thinking about the feelings of the women that I used. I didn't care."

Taking Taylor's hand, and kissing it he continued. "Mia, I apologize to you for my part in this. If I hadn't been trying to add to my body count...well, I'm sorry ok?"

Mia nodded, with her acceptance of his apology.

Taylor stared at Mia, Dain, and her brother. They were willing to let bygones be bygones, maybe she should also.

"Ok, I will let the past be the past. But Mia, if you hurt my brother I will hunt you down as if you were a rabid dog. Do we understand each other?"

"Yes Taylor we understand each other," Mia replied, embracing a smiling Kylon.

"Um, I take it everything is ok in here since I haven't heard any screaming or objects being thrown,"

Anderson asked, sticking his head through the doorway. They all laughed.

#

Jayden let himself out, after confirming that Kylon was indeed alive. He was on his way to the party when he heard the news of the crash. Hoping against hope that the report was wrong, he had let himself inside, just as Kylon professed his love for Mia and hers for him. He was relieved to see that all was well, but he too was surprised at Kylon's announcement.

His major reason for attending the party was to talk to Andee. Over time, he realized that he had made a mistake in breaking things off with her. Everyone was right; it wasn't Andee's fault that Mia had acted out nor was it her place to inform him of his sister's misdeeds. It wasn't his business or place to regulate Mia's or anyone else's life.

He had listened to his cousin profess his love and was about to go in search of Andee when he spotted her in the hallway with a man he did not know. He watched her and the man kissed each other passionately. He didn't know what to make of this. At first, he was angry but soon remembered that he had given up his right to be angry the moment he left her.

Taking one last look at the smiling couple, he pulled the door closed. He was walking back to his rental car when Anderson caught up with him.

"Jayden wait up," he called out to him. "Where are you going?"

"I'm headed back to the airport to catch a flight home. I wanted to make things right with Andee, but I see that I'm too late."

Anderson stuck his hands in his pockets, feeling bad for him. "You saw her with Tor, didn't you?"

"That's his name, Tor?" Anderson nodded. "Yeah, I saw her. Who is he?"

"She met him the day you deserted her. He was taken by her the moment he saw her and hasn't left her side since," Anderson informed his brother.

"She seems taken with him as well," Jayden commented.

Anderson looked down the street, not knowing what to say to him.

"Look, I know that I brought this on myself. I should have listened to you and thought about what I was doing." Jayden shook his head at his own foolishness. "I was so stubborn and self-righteous and it has cost me Andee," he added sadly.

"Tell her I wish the best for her. I mean that." Jayden clasped his brother's shoulder before he continued to his car. Anderson watched as he drove away, feeling badly for his brother. Turning to go back inside the house, he was startled by the appearance of Tor.

"Was that Jayden?" He asked Anderson watching the disappearing car.

"Yeah, it was," Anderson replied.

"I just want you to know that I will do whatever I can to make Andee happy. I care for her and plan to make her my wife in the near future. I don't want your brother interfering. He had his chance and he forfeited that chance the moment he walked out of her life. Andee is happy now and I want her to stay that way," Tor informed Anderson.

"My brother recognizes that, which is why he left. He doesn't want to bring any more grief to her life, Tor. He's aware that he messed up by letting her go, but accepts that she's moved on. So you don't have to worry about Jayden," Anderson assured him.

Tor hoped that was the case. He nodded once, indicating that he understood. Anderson nodded his response before he made his way back inside.

#

Jayden drove back to the airport deep in thought. He replayed the image of Andee kissing another man repeatedly in his mind. He had messed up big time and there was no way that he could fix it. Everyone told him that he was making a mistake, but he wouldn't listen. Before he left, he had looked around the room at the happy couples. There was his mother with Matthew, Anderson, and Paige, and even Mia with Kylon. Who could have seen that coming? He shook his head at that one. However, the couple that made the most impact was Andee and this person Tor.

After returning his rental car, Jayden was headed into the terminal when he spotted Rendell coming out. Curious to know why he was there, Jayden stopped him.

"What are you doing here?" He asked Rendell.

Surprised to see his son, Rendell smiled until he remembered their last encounter. "I was invited by Anderson and Taylor to Kylon's retirement party," He answered.

Anderson had decided that he had punished his father enough. His wife was right; people make mistakes and will continue to make them. He felt that Rendell was truly remorseful for the ones that he had made. Anderson had asked Taylor as well as his mother and stepfather if it were okay to include him in the celebration. They had all agreed provided Rendell stayed away from Adaisha.

Jayden turned Rendell's answer over in his mind before speaking. He was done playing judge and jury. Who was he to criticize considering his behavior had cost him Andee?

"That's good. I hope that you have a good time," he told his father before attempting to leave.

"Son...Jayden? Is everything ok?" Rendell asked a disheartened Jayden.

"No. I did something stupid that has cost me the woman that I love," he answered, rubbing his hand across his forehead.

Rendell sighed. He knew all too well what that felt like. "Where are you headed?" He asked.

"I'm going back home. There is nothing here for me anymore."

He couldn't bear the thought of staying a minute longer than he had to. Even though his brother lived there, his only real reason for coming had been Andee, and now that was gone.

"Come, let's go find a restaurant with a bar and have some dinner before you catch your flight. What do you say?" Rendell asked his youngest son.

"Sure why not?" Jayden followed his father into the terminal. What did he have to lose?

Epilogue

Six months later

"Oh Paige you are so big, but you look great though," Dani added laughing, after Paige gave her the evil eye because of her 'big' remark.

"I must agree, with the looking great part. Pregnancy looks good on you," Andee also commented.

"Well thanks, ladies, but I feel huge. I can't believe that I have three more months before I deliver. What will I look like then?" She asked her two best friends.

"You are going to look wonderful, my love," Anderson told his pregnant wife. He kissed her to reinforce his point. "We are ready for the steaks if you ladies are finished preparing them." They were all at Anderson and Paige's home for a cookout to celebrate Dain and Taylor's engagement.

"Here you go." Dani handed the platter of meat to Anderson. "Has everyone shown up?" She asked him.

"Let's see, I think everyone is here except the guests of honor, but they just called. They're on their way." Anderson answered.

"Hi everyone," Mia spoke as she and Kylon entered the kitchen from the backyard. "How can we help?"

Everyone greeted the couple as they entered. Although Taylor was skeptical about Kylon and Mia's relationship, she had to admit that she had never seen her brother so happy. And as for Mia, she seemed to be smitten with Kylon. After they professed their love for each other, Mia had been the perfect citizen.

"Why don't you stir the sauce for the spaghetti," Andee told her.

Mia washed her hands and took to her appointed task. She was grateful to be a part of this happy group, especially after her appalling behavior towards Dain and Taylor. She was very grateful that they accepted her.

"So what's in the pots?" Kylon asked as he tried to lift a lid, only to be stopped by a hand slap from Dani.

"You will have to wait just like everyone else," she told him.

"Ok, ok, I am out of here. Kylon kissed Mia and left to join the men in the backyard.

"Hello, hello, sorry we're late," Dain greeted the group in the kitchen. He and Taylor had arrived.

"Yes, sorry for being late, but we had to pick up my engagement ring," Taylor explained raising her hand. She was all smiles as the women gathered around her.

"Hey, why has everyone gathered in here? I thought the party was outside; and where are those steaks? Tor has the grill ready," Devin addressed the room.

Kissing his wife again and grabbing the platter of steaks, Anderson answered. "I am right behind you. Come on Dain let's get this party started."

Kissing Taylor, Dain followed Anderson out to the backyard.

"Have you set a date?" Andee asked Taylor.

"No not yet, but it will be soon. We love each other and we don't see why we should wait," Taylor told her friends.

"Well, I for one am happy for both of you. I never thought that my brother would ever settle down with one woman let alone get married. I have never seen him so happy." Dani was all smiles.

"You and Devin have been together for a while, when do you two plan to jump the broom?" Taylor asked her.

Dani shrugged. "We feel we don't need a piece of paper to define our love. I know that our way isn't for everyone, but it's how we feel."

Paige and Andee exchanged glances. They had known Dani most of their lives and had taken it for granted that she, like every other woman they knew, wanted the dream of marriage and a family. They both wondered if it was Devin's idea not to get married. They planned to get to the bottom of it later.

"What about you and Tor, have you two made any plans?" Dani asked Andee readily changing the subject.

"Actually, we have," she told them. "We were going to announce it a little later, but since you asked."

Andee wiped her hands before she reached into her purse. After a couple of moments of searching, she pulled out her wedding rings and placed them on her finger before she showed her friends.

"We got married yesterday," she told them with a squeal.

"OMG!" Are you kidding me?" Paige asked a grinning Andee. The women were ecstatic. They each gathered around Andee to hug her and congratulate her on her marriage.

#

Hearing the excitement from the kitchen, the men looked towards the house.

"I wonder what that's all about," Dain casually commented.

After taking a swallow from his beer bottle, Tor answered him. "Andee probably told them that she's my wife," he said nonchalantly.

The men looked at each other before they turned toward Tor.

"Wife? What do you mean wife?" Devin asked with a perplexed expression, with the other men in the yard asking the same.

Placing his bottle on the picnic table, Tor lifted his left hand to display his platinum wedding band. "We got married yesterday," he told them with a broad grin.

The men shook Tor's hand and pounded his back with congratulations.

"Man, how did you beat me to the altar?" Dain asked. He was shaking his head. After meeting at Kylon's retirement party, he and Tor had become good friends; bonding over the Mia mess.

"I don't believe in wasting time when it comes to important things." Smiling he added, "Andee has become the most important person in my life. I love her; she loves me. We didn't see a need to wait," Tor shared with friends.

Kylon clasped him on the back. "I'm happy for you man. Who knew by me hiring you, that you would end up married to Andee." He shook his head. "Life sure is strange.

"And speaking of that, I guess I owe you an apology," Tor confessed.

"Yeah, how so?" Kylon asked, taking a pull from his beer.

"I didn't think that you and Mia would work out. You know that I thought the woman was nuts, but since you two have been together, she has changed completely. I guess love can turn some people around," Tor told him.

"Tor you weren't the only one who thought that," Dain chimed in. "I had my reservations also. Kylon, you are a miracle worker," He added with a chuckle.

"Hey, hey now, that's my sister you're talking about," Anderson joked.

Kylon laughed. "No fellas, I understand. She was a handful, but all Mia needed was a man who could reach her emotionally. She was only acting out because she needed to be loved and not treated like an object. I don't think that she fully understood it herself. She was searching for something she couldn't name and I'm just grateful that I'm able to give that to her." He and Anderson tapped beer bottles in agreement.

"Devin, when are you and Dani going to tie that knot? You two have been dating for a while" Anderson asked.

Devin was enjoying the good humor that they were engaged in, but when the focus turned on him, he was hesitant. He had asked Dani to marry him several times and each time she said that she didn't feel that marriage was necessary for them. He loved her and wanted to be her husband, but for some reason, she didn't want to marry him.

"What can I say, I love her. I guess we will get around to it." That was all that he could say. He couldn't explain it to them when he didn't understand himself.

Sensing that this was a sore subject, Anderson changed the topics. Devin nodded his appreciation as he turned back to the steaks on the grill.

#

"So this is why you wanted the day off yesterday? Andee, where did all of this happen? Why didn't you have a wedding? We could have planned a beautiful ceremony," Paige was asking the questions they all wanted the answers to.

Laughing, Andee answered, "We decided to just, do it. We had a small ceremony in the park by the lake. Ladies, I love him more than I could have imagined. We took our relationship slow, learning each other along the way. With the sex thing not on the table, it made the journey just that much sweeter. There wasn't any pressure, only our enjoyment of each other. And to answer your question about a wedding, that wasn't my thing. I just wanted my man and that's all." She ended with a grin.

"I have one question," Taylor said. "Have you finally consummated your relationship?"

"Yes, and I must say it was well worth the wait. I feel I have become one with my husband. I truly understand that phrase now. It was beautiful. So I am sure that you ladies will understand if we have to leave early. We are on our honeymoon you know."

They all laughed.

* 9 7 8 0 6 1 5 6 6 4 9 5 8 *